LE CHARROI DE NIMES

TRADUCTIONS DES CLASSIQUES FRANÇAIS
DU MOYEN AGE
sous la direction de Jean Dufournet
XI

FABIENNE GÉGOU

LE CHARROI DE NIMES

CHANSON DE GESTE ANONYME
DU XIIe SIÈCLE

TRADUCTION

PARIS
LIBRAIRIE HONORÉ CHAMPION, ÉDITEUR
7, QUAI MALAQUAIS (VIe)
1980

ISBN 2-85203-014-4
© ÉDITIONS CHAMPION - 1980 - PARIS

AVANT-PROPOS

La traduction de cette chanson de geste présente des difficultés et même des écueils. En effet chaque érudit a une opinion personnelle bien définie quant au sens à donner à certains passages, à certaines expressions, à certains clichés épiques ; notre travail ne peut donc satisfaire l'un qu'en recevant la critique de l'autre. Le Charroi de Nîmes a été mainte fois étudié dans tous ses détails depuis plus d'un siècle, a fait l'objet d'arrangements, parfois de valeur, tel celui d'Alfred Jeanroy[1]. Enfin, il n'existe encore aucune bonne édition que l'on puisse traduire en

1. *La geste de Guillaume Fierebrace et de Raynouart au tinel,* dans *Poèmes et récits de la Vieille France,* t. VI, Paris, de Boccard, 1924.

toute sécurité ; n'ayant à notre disposition que celle de Perrier[2], nous l'avons prise comme point de départ de notre traduction, mais avec d'infinies précautions, étant donné sa médiocrité. Toutefois, nous avons pu compenser, en partie, ses insuffisances grâce à trois articles qui signalent les réfections les plus urgentes à apporter au texte (repris par un chercheur italien) et au glossaire[3] ; en ce qui concerne ce dernier, il est non seulement inexact en bien des cas, mais il contient si peu de mots qu'il apporte une

2. *Le Charroi de Nîmes, chanson de geste du XIIe siècle*, Paris, Champion, C.F.M.A., 1931 (seconde impression en 1968).

3. Nous avons utilisé pour améliorer le texte de Perrier et pour obtenir, de ce fait, une traduction plus satisfaisante de nombreux passages, l'article de Cl. Régnier, *A propos de l'édition du « Charroi de Nîmes »*, dans l'*Information littéraire*, 20e année, janvier-février 1968, no 1, p. 32-33. Nous avons complété les judicieuses remarques de Cl. Régnier grâce à un compte rendu et à une réponse à G.E. Sansone, parus dans la *Romania*, respectivement aux fascicules 1 et 3 du t. 91, Paris, 1970, et rédigés par D. McMillan dont une édition du *Charroi* est sous presse.

aide pratiquement nulle au lecteur ; cependant, l'index des noms propres est plus satisfaisant.

N'étant ni éditeur ni commentateur, notre rôle n'est pas d'éclaircir les questions relatives à l'auteur ou à la composition du poème dont se sont occupés et s'occupent encore de nombreux médiévistes. Disons seulement que dans l'enchaînement chronologique des faits, le Charroi *se place après le* Couronnement de Louis *et avant la* Prise d'Orange *; on pense toutefois qu'il a existé une* Prise d'Orange *primitive connue du rédacteur du* Charroi *et que nous ne possédons maintenant qu'une* Prise d'Orange *renouvelée écrite pour compléter l'ensemble* Couronnement-Charroi. *Nous sommes en tous cas en présence d'une trilogie à la mode antique qui représente le noyau central du cycle de Guillaume, et notre tâche est de rendre aussi accessible que faire se peut au lecteur contemporain la seconde partie de cette trilogie. On date le* Charroi *au plus tôt de 1135 et au plus tard de 1165 ; l'auteur enfin est anonyme et nous n'avons actuellement aucun moyen* *de le faire sortir de cet anonymat*[4]. *Une discussion précise de ces problèmes sortirait du cadre de cet Avant-Propos.*

Nous nous bornerons donc à situer notre chanson par rapport au récit précédent puis à caractériser ses principaux traits narratifs. Dans le premier épisode du Couronnement, *on assiste à la cérémonie durant laquelle Louis, fils de Charlemagne, reçoit la couronne grâce à l'énergique intervention de Guillaume ; dans le second épisode, Guillaume tue le géant Corsolt, en combat singulier, sous les murs de Rome et sauve ainsi des Sarrasins la Ville Eternelle et le pape ; dans le troisième épisode, Guillaume châtie le traître Acelin qui voulait ravir la couronne à Louis et réprime un soulèvement des seigneurs du Nord ; dans le dernier épisode enfin, notre héros retourne à Rome pour combattre Gui l'Allemand qui s'était rendu maître de la ville, et après l'avoir tué, il fait couronner Louis empereur. Toutes ces aventures sont rappelées dans le cours du* Charroi,

4. Cf. J. Frappier, *Les Chansons de geste du cycle de Guillaume d'Orange*, Paris, S.E.D.E.S., 1967, t. II, p. 28 et 186.

si bien que sans connaître le Couronnement le public médiéval pouvait entendre chanter le Charroi de Nîmes *avec un plaisir sans mélange.*

Le Charroi, *quant à lui, comporte trois chapitres que nous avons matériellement indiqués dans notre traduction pour plus de clarté :* La colère de Guillaume, L'expédition, La prise de Nîmes. *L'inspiration de la chanson se fonde sur trois thèmes épiques :* l'ingratitude de Louis, la conquête d'un fief en terre sarrasine, *enfin* l'esprit de croisade contre l'infidèle, la défense de la foi chrétienne, *ressort de propagande commun aux chansons de geste qui appartiennent à la « poésie militante*[5] ». *En ce qui regarde la critique interne du poème, son allure héroï-comique a provoqué de nombreux commentaires ; remarquons notamment que, si F. Lot constate qu'il y a déjà du Corneille dans le* Charroi, *J. Frappier note qu'une fois l'expédition commencée, « le récit rappellerait plutôt Alexandre Dumas » ce qui n'est pas pour déplaire*[6].

5. Cf. J. Frappier, *op. cit.*, p. 121 et 191.

6. Cf. J. Frappier, *op. cit.*, p. 193 ; cf. aussi F. Lot, dans *Romania*, XXVI, 1897, p. 568.

*Nous sommes personnellement très inté-
ressé, dans la partie dite comique ou même
triviale du* Charroi *qui commence avec la
rencontre du vilain pour se terminer quand
Guillaume abandonne son rôle de marchand,
par tout ce que ce passage étendu nous apprend
sur la civilisation matérielle du milieu du
XII*e *siècle : la vie quotidienne du paysan,
le prix du pain, la confection d'un tonneau,
la nature des riches produits offerts par un
marchand ambulant, l'octroi, la sécurité pro-
mise à l'étranger en situation régulière ;
l'énumération « exotique » des places d'Europe
qui permettent d'amasser une fortune est
également instructive.*

À l'exception des premiers vers du Couronnement, *la trilogie est sans fondement
historique : le* Charroi de Nîmes, *comme la*
Prise d'Orange, *est entièrement imaginaire
et ne cherche qu'à exalter un héros idéal
aux yeux des seigneurs du XII*e *siècle ; la
longueur des trois chansons est en harmonie,
bien que le* Charroi *soit la plus courte des
trois*[7]. *Ajoutons pour terminer que le texte*

7. Tandis que le *Couronnement de Louis* a une
étendue de 2695 vers (éd. Langlois) et la *Prise d'Orange*.

de ce poème se lit essentiellement dans huit manuscrits dont cinq sont à Paris : B.N. fr. 774 (A1), B.N. fr. 1449 (A2), B.N. fr. 368 (A3)[8], B.N. fr. 1448 (D), B.N. fr. 24369-70 (B2), un à Milan : Bibl. Trivulzienne, 1025 (A4), un à Londres : British Museum, Roy. 20 D XI (B1), un à Boulogne-sur-Mer, Bibl. communale, S. Bertin 192 (C).

Remercions ici notre maître, le professeur Félix Lecoy, que nous avons consulté sur certains points et qui a accueilli nos questions avec la plus grande bienveillance.

F.G.

de 1888 vers (éd. Régnier), le *Charroi de Nîmes* contient 1486 vers (éd. Perrier).

8. Nous adoptons les sigles de Cl. Régnier dans son édition de la *Prise d'Orange :* A3 pour le manuscrit de Paris, B.N., fr. 368, et A4 pour le manuscrit de Milan, à l'inverse de l'édition Perrier du *Charroi.*

La colère de Guillaume

I

Écoutez, seigneurs, que Dieu accroisse votre
valeur,
Le glorieux, le roi de majesté !
Vous plaît-il d'entendre une belle chanson
Sur le meilleur homme qui ait jamais cru
en Dieu ?
Il s'agit de Guillaume, le marquis au court
nez,
Et de la manière dont il prit Nîmes en condui-
sant le Charroi* ;
Plus tard il conquit la cité d'Orange,
Fit conférer le baptême à Guibourc
Après l'avoir ravie au roi Thibaut l'Esclerc*,
10 Puis l'épousa en mariage légitime*.

L'astérisque renvoie aux notes, numérotées selon les vers.

Sous les murs de Rome, dans la prairie, il tua
                                    Corsolt*.
Il rehaussa beaucoup la sainte chrétienté
Et fit tant sur terre qu'il est couronné aux cieux.
C'était en mai, au renouveau de l'été* ;
Les bois se parent de feuilles, les prés rever-
                                    dissent,
Les oiseaux chantent joliment et harmonieu-
                                    sement.
Le comte Guillaume revenait de chasser
Dans une forêt où il était resté longtemps.
Il avait pris deux cerfs de prime graisse
20 Qu'il avait soigneusement chargés sur trois
                                    mulets d'Espagne.
Le baron avait quatre flèches pendues à son
                                    côté ;
Il rapportait de la chasse son arc de cytise.
En sa compagnie se trouvaient quarante jeunes
                                    gens,
Fils de comtes et de princes pourvus de fiefs ;
Ils étaient, depuis peu, armés chevaliers.
Ils tiennent des oiseaux pour passer agréable-
                                    ment le temps,
Et font mener avec eux leurs meutes.
Ils sont entrés à Paris par le Petit-Pont.

Le comte Guillaume était très noble et très
                                    vaillant*.

30 Il fit porter sa venaison chez lui.

En chemin il a rencontré Bertrand ;
Il lui demande : « Mon neveu, d'où venez-
vous ? »
Bertrand répond : « Voici la vérité :
Je viens du palais où je suis resté longtemps ;
J'y ai beaucoup écouté et entendu.
Notre empereur a donné des fiefs à ses barons :
A celui-ci une terre, à celui-là un château,
à cet autre une cité,
A cet autre encore une ville, distribuant selon
sa compétence ;
Vous et moi, mon oncle, sommes oubliés.
40   Pour moi qui suis un jeune homme, cela ne
fait rien,
Mais pour vous, seigneur, qui êtes si vaillant,
Qui vous êtes tant fatigué et dépensé
A veiller la nuit et à jeûner le jour... ! »
A ces mots, Guillaume a éclaté de rire :
« Mon neveu, dit le comte, laissez tout cela.
Allez vite chez vous
Et équipez-vous convenablement ;
Moi j'irai parler à Louis. »
Bertrand répond : « Seigneur, je suis à vos
ordres. »
50   Il regagne rapidement sa demeure.

Le comte Guillaume était très noble et très
vaillant.

Il se rend au palais d'une traite,

Descend de cheval sous l'olivier rameux,
Puis gravit l'escalier de marbre*.
Il a traversé la salle avec une telle impétuosité
Qu'il rompt les tiges de ses souliers de cuir ;
Tous les barons en sont effrayés.
A sa vue, le roi s'est levé pour aller à sa rencontre,
Puis il lui a dit : « Guillaume, asseyez-vous donc.
60 — Non merci, Sire, répond Guillaume le vaillant,
Je voudrais seulement vous dire un mot. »
Alors Louis : « Je suis à vos ordres.
A mon avis, vous serez écouté comme il faut*.
— Louis, mon frère, dit Guillaume le vaillant,
Je t'ai beaucoup servi, non pas en te massant*,
Ni en dépouillant de leur héritage la veuve et le jeune enfant,
Mais je t'ai servi avec mes armes comme un baron ;
Pour toi, j'ai livré mainte rude bataille rangée
Où j'ai tué maint noble jeune homme,
70 Péché dont je porte le poids.
Quels qu'ils fussent, Dieu les avait créés.
Que Dieu prenne soin de leurs âmes et qu'Il me pardonne !
— Seigneur Guillaume, dit Louis le vaillant,
De grâce, patientez un peu.
L'hiver passera et l'été reviendra :

L'un de ces jours mourra l'un de mes pairs ;
Je vous donnerai toutes ses terres,
Et aussi sa femme si vous voulez l'épouser. »
A ces mots, peu s'en faut que Guillaume ne
soit fou de colère :
80 « Dieu qui fut supplicié sur la croix ! dit le
comte,
Comme l'attente est longue pour le pauvre
garçon
Qui n'a rien à prendre pour lui ni rien à donner
à autrui !
J'ai mon cheval à nourrir,
Et je ne sais pas encore où trouver son grain*.
Dieu ! quel val profond doit dévaler
Et quelle haute montagne doit monter
Celui qui attend sa richesse de la mort d'un
autre ! »

II

« Dieu ! dit Guillaume, comme l'attente est
longue ici
Pour un garçon de mon âge !
90 Il n'a rien à donner à autrui ni rien à prendre
pour lui.
Il me faut donner sa provende à mon fougueux
cheval :
Je ne sais pas encore où prendre l'avoine.
Crois-tu, roi, que je ne me lamente pas ? »

III

« Seigneur Louis, dit Guillaume le fier,
Si je n'avais pas craint de passer pour un
                fourbe auprès de mes compagnons*,
Il y a bien un an que je t'aurais laissé,
Quand de Spolète me sont parvenues les lettres
Que m'envoya le puissant roi Gaiffier :
De son royaume il me donnerait une part,
100   Une moitié tout entière avec sa fille.
(Et si en épousant la fille, j'avais acquis un
                très vaste domaine,)
J'aurais pu faire la guerre au roi de France*. »
A ces mots, le roi croit perdre l'esprit.
Il prononce des paroles qu'il aurait bien dû
                retenir.
Dès lors, le mal commence à s'aggraver,
La colère à devenir plus forte entre eux.

IV

« Seigneur Guillaume, dit le roi Louis,
Il n'y a personne à travers tout ce pays,
Gaiffier ou un autre, pas plus que le roi de
                Spolète,
Qui osât accepter l'hommage d'un seul de mes
                sujets,

110 Sans qu'avant un an écoulé il fût tué ou
                                          pris
     Ou chassé de ses terres et exilé.
     — Dieu ! dit le comte, comme je suis maltraité
     En étant réduit à l'état de prisonnier à cause
                                de ma pitance* !
     Si je vous rends service désormais, que je sois
                                déshonoré ! »

                         V

     « Nobles compagnons, dit Guillaume le vail-
                                          lant,
     Retournez vite dans ma demeure,
     Équipez-vous convenablement
     Et chargez les bagages sur les bêtes de somme.
     De colère il me faut quitter la cour.
120 Puisque pour subsister, nous sommes restés
                                avec le roi,
     Il peut dire qu'il a fait un fameux coup ! »
     Ses gens répondent : « Nous sommes à vos
                                ordres. »
     Guillaume est monté sur la pierre du foyer,
     S'est appuyé un peu sur l'arc de cytise
     Qu'il avait apporté de la chasse,
     Avec une telle force qu'il l'a brisé par le milieu
     Et que les morceaux en volent jusqu'aux pou-
                                          tres,
     Puis tombent devant le nez du roi.

Alors Guillaume, oubliant toute mesure, com-
mença à parler
130   A Louis, car il l'avait beaucoup servi :
« Mes grands services vont être mis sous vos
yeux,
Les grands combats et les batailles rangées.
Seigneur Louis, dit Guillaume le vaillant,
Ne te souviens-tu pas du rude combat
Que j'ai livré pour toi sous les murs de Rome
dans la prairie ?
Là, j'ai lutté contre l'émir Corsolt,
L'homme le plus fort que l'on pût trouver
Dans la chrétienté ou sur la terre des païens.
De sa lame d'épée nue il m'asséna un tel coup
140   Sur mon heaume aux pierreries serties
d'or
Qu'il en fit tomber le cristal* par terre.
Il coupa le nasal protégeant mon nez
Et fit glisser sa lame jusqu'à mes narines ;
Il me fallut soutenir* le bout de mon nez
avec mes deux mains ;
Il y eut une grande bosse quand on sutura
la plaie.
Maudit soit le médecin qui me soigna !
C'est pour cela que l'on m'appelle Guillaume
au court nez*.
J'en ai grand dépit quand je parais entre
mes compagnons
Et devant le roi quand j'accomplis mon service.

150   Personne n'en retira épieu,
      Heaume, bouclier, palefroi ferré
      Ou lame d'acier avec son pommeau. »

                        VI

      « Roi Louis, dit Guillaume le sage,
      Loyal empereur, vous êtes le fils de Charles,
      Du meilleur roi qui portât jamais les armes,
      Du plus fier et du plus juste.
      Roi, qu'il te souvienne d'une sauvage bataille
      Que je livrai pour toi au gué de Pierrelate* :
      Je fis prisonnier Dagobert qui restera auprès
                                        de vous.
160   Voyez-le avec ces opulentes fourrures de
                                        martre ;
      S'il le nie, je dois en être blâmé.
      Après ce combat, j'en livrai un autre pour toi :
      Quand Charlemagne voulut te faire roi,
      Alors que la couronne était posée sur l'autel,
      Tu restas longtemps agenouillé sans bouger ;
      Les Français virent que tu n'avais pas beau-
                                        coup de valeur :
      Ils voulaient faire de toi un clerc, un abbé
                                        ou un prêtre,
      Ou bien ils t'auraient nommé chanoine quelque
                                        part.
      Alors dans la chapelle Marie-Madeleine*,

170 Arnéïs, en raison de sa puissante famille,
Voulut tirer la couronne à lui.
Quand je le vis, cela ne me plut pas :
Je lui donnai un grand coup sur la nuque
Et l'abattis à la renverse sur le sol de marbre ;
Pour cet acte, je fus pris en haine par sa
puissante famille.
Je m'avançai de toute la largeur de la cour
royale
Si bien que tout le monde le vit,
Ainsi que le pape et tous les patriarches ;
Je pris la couronne et vous l'avez gardée
depuis*.
180 Vous ne vous souvenez guère de ce service
Quand vous distribuez vos terres sans penser
à moi ! »

VII

« Seigneur Louis, dit Guillaume le preux,
Ne te souvient-il pas de l'infâme orgueilleux
Qui vint te défier ici, en ta cour ?
« Tu n'as aucun droit sur la France », dit-il
devant tous.
Tu n'eus pas un seul baron dans ton empire,
Légitime empereur, pour dire oui ou non,
Quand je me souvins de mon seigneur naturel.
Je m'avançai, et agissant plutôt comme un
insensé,

190   Je le tuai* avec un pieu comme un traître.

Puis arriva un moment où j'éprouvai une
grande peur,

Quand je revins du Mont Saint-Michel

Et que je rencontrai Richard le vieux, le roux.

C'était le père de l'orgueilleux Normand ;

Il avait une troupe de vingt hommes et je
n'en avais que deux ;

Je tirai l'épée et me comportai courageu-
sement :

Avec ma lame nue je tuai sept des leurs ;

Sous les yeux des autres, je désarçonnai leur
seigneur.

Je te le livrai à Paris, à ta cour ;

200   Plus tard, il mourut dans ta grande
tour*.

Vous ne vous souvenez pas beaucoup de ce
service

Quand vous donnez des terres sans penser
à moi.

Roi, souviens-toi donc de Gui l'Allemand :

Quand tu te rendais à Saint-Pierre de Rome,

Il te réclama les Français, les Bourguignons,

La couronne et la cité de Laon.

Je combattis contre lui, ce que virent de
nombreux barons,

Et je lui passai ma lance avec le gonfalon
au travers du corps,

Puis je le lançai dans le Tibre, et les poissons
le mangèrent.

210   De cette affaire, je me serais tenu pour
fou,

Mais je vins trouver mon hôte Gui⁻

Qui me fit fuir par mer sur un navire*.

Roi, souviens-toi donc de la puissante armée
d'Oton* :

Avec toi il y avait les Français, les Bourguignons,

Les Lorrains, les Flamands et les Frisons.

Vous avez traversé le Grand-Saint-Bernard,
vous êtes passés à Montbardon,

Puis vous êtes allés à Rome, au lieu dit le
Parc de Néron* ;

Moi-même, en personne, je dressai ta tente,

Puis je te servis une excellente venaison. »

VIII

220   « Quand tu eus terminé ton repas,

Je vins te trouver pour prendre congé.

Tu me l'accordas bien volontiers,

Croyant que j'allais m'allonger

Sous ma tente pour me reposer.

Je fis mettre en selle deux mille chevaliers,

Et je vins veiller à ta sûreté, en arrière de ta
tente,

Dans un petit bois de pins et de lauriers :

Là je fis s'embusquer les guerriers.

Tu ne daignas pas prendre garde à ceux
de Rome ;

230 Ils étaient plus de quinze mille à cheval,

Et ils arrivèrent devant ta tente pour lancer
des traits,

En rompre les câbles et la renverser,

Tirer tes nappes et répandre ta nourriture ;

Je vis ton sénéchal et ton portier prisonniers ;

De tente en tente tu t'enfuyais à pied

A travers les rangs serrés des combattants,
comme un pauvre chien.

Tu t'es écrié à voix très haute :

« Bertrand, Guillaume, venez ici, secourez-
moi ! »

J'éprouvai alors pour toi, seigneur roi, une
très grande pitié.

240 Je combattis là contre sept mille guerriers
bien équipés,

Et je fis prisonniers pour toi plus de trois cents

Chevaliers aux fougueux destriers.

Je vis leur seigneur baissé contre un mur* :

Je le reconnus très bien à son solide heaume
renforcé de bandes,

Et à l'escarboucle qui brillait sur son nasal.

Je lui donnai un tel coup de mon épieu tran-
chant

Que je l'abattis sur l'encolure de son destrier.

Il cria grâce et j'en eus pitié :

« Baron, ne me tue pas, si tu es Guillaume ! »
250   Je te l'ai amené sans retard*.
De ce fait, tu as encore à Rome un fief impor-
tant.
Tu es puissant maintenant, et moi je suis
peu estimé.
Aussi longtemps que je t'ai servi, je t'ai aidé,
Je n'y ai pas gagné un dernier vaillant
Et les Picards me surnomment Sire le « traîne
en cour* ».

IX

« Seigneur Louis, a poursuivi Guillaume,
Je t'ai servi si longtemps que j'ai blanchi
Et je n'y ai pas gagné un fétu vaillant,
De quoi être mieux vêtu à ta cour* ;
260   Je ne sais pas encore de quel côté tourne
ma porte* !
Seigneur Louis, qu'est devenu ton esprit ?
On avait coutume de dire que j'étais ton
favori ;
Je chevauchais de beaux chevaux à longue
crinière,
Et je te servais par les champs et les marais.
Jamais personne n'a reçu quelque avantage
à la suite de cela
Et n'a eu un clou en plus dans son bouclier
A moins que la lance d'autrui ne l'ait frappé
durement* !

J'ai tué plus de vingt mille Turcs infidèles ;
A l'avenir, au nom de Celui qui règne là-haut
                                        dans le ciel,
270   Je me retournerai contre mon suzerain.
Vous pourrez faire que je ne sois plus votre
                                        ami ! »

X

« Dieu né de la sainte Vierge, dit Guillaume,
Pourquoi ai-je tué tant de beaux jeunes gens
Et pourquoi ai-je endeuillé tant de mères,
Si bien que le péché est resté dans mon cœur* ?
J'ai tant servi ce mauvais roi de France,
Et je n'y ai pas gagné la valeur d'un fer de
                                        lance ! »

XI

« Seigneur Guillaume, répondit Louis le
                                        vaillant,
Par l'apôtre que l'on va prier au Parc de Néron,
280   Il reste encore soixante de vos pairs
Auxquels je n'ai rien promis ni donné. »
Et Guillaume lui dit : « Seigneur roi, vous
                                        mentez.
Je n'ai pas de pair dans la chrétienté,
A l'exception de vous-même qui êtes couronné.
Je ne cherche pas à me vanter à vos dépens.

Maintenant prenez ceux que vous avez nom-
més,
Conduisez-les l'un après l'autre dans une
prairie
Sur des chevaux équipés et armés ;
Si je ne vous en ai pas tué tant et plus,
290   Je ne veux absolument rien de vos biens,
Et je me mesurerai avec vous-même, si vous
voulez y aller. »
Après l'avoir entendu, le roi a baissé la tête
devant lui ;
Puis il s'est redressé et a ainsi parlé :

XII

« Seigneur Guillaume, dit Louis le noble,
Maintenant, je le vois bien, tu es rempli de
colère.
— C'est vrai, dit Guillaume, selon l'habitude
de ma famille.
Il en va ainsi quand on est au service de
mauvaises gens :
Plus on en fait, moins on en tire ;
Au contraire, les choses vont continuellement
en se gâtant. »

XIII

300   « Seigneur Guillaume, dit Louis le preux,

Maintenant, je le vois bien, vous êtes très
en colère.
— C'est vrai, dit Guillaume, tout comme
mes ancêtres.
Il en va ainsi quand on est au service d'un
mauvais seigneur :
Plus on le sert, moins on en tire.
— Seigneur Guillaume, lui répond Louis,
Vous m'avez protégé et servi avec amour
Plus que personne qui soit à ma cour.
Avancez, je vous donnerai un beau présent :
Prenez le domaine du valeureux comte Foul-
que ;
310 Trois mille hommes vous serviront.
— Je n'en ferai rien, Sire, lui répond Guil-
laume.
Le noble comte a laissé deux enfants
Qui pourront gérer son domaine convenable-
ment.
Donnez m'en un autre, car je ne me soucie
pas de celui-là. »

XIV

« Seigneur Guillaume, dit le roi Louis,
Puisque vous ne voulez pas vous occuper
de ce domaine
Et puisque vous ne voulez pas l'ôter aux
enfants,

Prenez le domaine du Bourguignon Auberi
Et épousez sa marâtre Hermensant de Tori,
320   La meilleure femme qui ait jamais bu de
vin* ;
Trois mille soldats habillés de fer vous servi-
ront.
— Je n'en ferai rien, Sire, répondit Guillaume.
Le noble comte a laissé un fils :
Son nom est Robert, mais il est tout petit ;
Il ne sait pas encore mettre ses chausses et
ses vêtements.
Si Dieu lui accorde de devenir grand et
robuste,
Il pourra gérer tout le domaine convena-
blement. »

XV

« Seigneur Guillaume, dit Louis le fier,
Puisque tu ne veux pas dépouiller cet enfant,
330   Prends donc le domaine du marquis Béran-
ger.
Le comte est mort, épouse sa femme ;
Deux mille chevaliers te serviront,
Aux armes brillantes et aux destriers rapides ;
De ton bien, ils n'auront pas un denier vail-
lant*. »
A ces mots, Guillaume pense perdre la raison ;
De sa voix claire, il commence à crier :

« Écoutez-moi, nobles chevaliers,
Voilà comment est protégé par Louis, mon
                                  juste seigneur,
Celui qui le sert avec dévouement.
340 Je vais vous parler du marquis Béranger :
Il était né au val de Riviers* ;
Il tua un comte, ne put s'acquitter de ce
                                  meurtre*
Et vint en courant à Mont-Laon, au trône
                                  impérial ;
Là, il tomba aux pieds de l'empereur,
Qui le reçut de bon gré,
Lui donna un domaine et une épouse noble.
L'autre le servit longtemps sans faute.
Puis il arriva que le roi fit la guerre
Aux Sarrasins, aux Turcs et aux Esclers.
350 La mêlée fut grande et terrible ;
Le roi fut jeté à bas de son destrier.
Jamais, au grand jamais, il n'y serait remonté,
Mais surgit le marquis Béranger.
Il vit son seigneur mal en point dans les rangs
                                  serrés des combattants :
Il se précipita de ce côté au galop de son cheval,
Ayant au poing sa lame d'acier fourbi.
Il fit là un carnage tel qu'en fait le sanglier
                                  au milieu des chiens,
Puis il descendit de son destrier rapide
Pour secourir et aider son seigneur.

360 Le roi monta à cheval tandis que le marquis
lui tenait l'étrier,

Et il s'enfuit tel un lévrier couard,

Alors que le marquis Béranger restait sur
place ;

Là, nous le vîmes tuer et dépecer

Sans pouvoir ni le secourir ni l'aider.

Il a laissé un noble héritier :

Ce dernier se nomme le petit Béranger.

Il est complètement fou celui qui veut faire
tort à l'enfant,

Aussi vrai que je demande l'aide de Dieu,
c'est un traître et un renégat.

L'empereur veut me donner son fief :

370 Je n'en veux pas ! Je tiens absolument à ce que
vous l'appreniez tous.

Et je dois absolument vous faire connaître
ceci :

Par l'apôtre que l'on va prier à Rome,

Il n'y a en France si hardi chevalier

Qui, s'il prend le domaine du petit Béranger,

Ne perde aussitôt la tête grâce à cette épée.

— Merci beaucoup, seigneur », disent les
chevaliers

Qui sont les proches de l'enfant Béranger.

Ils sont cent qui le saluent de la tête,

Qui tous vont embrasser ses genoux.

380 « Seigneur Guillaume, dit Louis, écoutez :

Puisqu'il ne vous convient pas de prendre
                                    ce domaine,
Aussi vrai que je demande l'aide de Dieu,
                    je vous offrirai maintenant un fief tel
Que, si vous êtes raisonnable, vous deviendrez
                                    très puissant.
Je vous donnerai un quart de la France,
Une abbaye sur quatre et aussi un marché
                                    sur quatre,
Une cité sur quatre et un archevêché sur
                                    quatre,
Un homme d'arme sur quatre et un chevalier
                                    sur quatre,
Un vavasseur sur quatre et un valet* sur
                                    quatre,
Une jeune fille sur quatre et une femme sur
                                    quatre,
390   Un prêtre sur quatre et aussi une église sur
                                    quatre ;
De mes écuries, je vous donne un destrier sur
                                    quatre,
De mon trésor, je vous donne un denier sur
                                    quatre ;
Je vous concède volontiers le quart
De tout l'empire que j'ai à gouverner.
Recevez-le, noble chevalier.
— Je n'en ferai rien, Sire, répondit Guillaume.
Je ne l'accepterais pas pour tout l'or du monde,
Car bientôt, ces vaillants chevaliers diraient :

« Voyez Guillaume, le marquis au fier visage,
400   Comme il a fait tort maintenant à son seigneur
                                    légitime ;
Ce dernier lui a complètement concédé la
                           moitié de son royaume,
Et Guillaume ne lui en paie pas un denier
                                    vaillant.
Il lui a maintenant rogné sérieusement sa
                                subsistance. »

XVI

« Seigneur Guillaume, dit Louis le vaillant,
Par l'apôtre que l'on va prier au Parc de Néron,
Puisque vous ne voulez pas recevoir ce fief,
Je ne sais que vous donner sur mon domaine
Et je ne sais pas non plus décider d'un autre
                                    don.
— Roi, dit Guillaume, laissez donc tout cela ;
410   Pour cette fois, je ne souhaite pas en parler
                                davantage.
Quand il vous plaira, vous me donnerez en
                           grand nombre
Châteaux et provinces, donjons et forteresses. »
Après ces mots, le comte est parti ;
Plein de rancœur, il descend l'escalier.
En chemin, il rencontre Bertrand
Qui lui demande : « Mon oncle, d'où venez-
                                vous ? »

Et Guillaume répond : « Je vais te parler
franchement :
Je viens de ce palais-là et j'y suis resté long-
temps.
Je me suis mis en colère et j'ai menacé Louis ;
420 Je l'ai servi sans limite, et il ne m'a rien
donné. »
Bertrand s'écrie : « Malédiction de Dieu !
Vous ne devez pas provoquer votre légitime
seigneur,
Mais le servir et l'honorer,
Le protéger et le défendre contre tous les
hommes.
— Allons donc ! répond Guillaume, il m'a
amené à un point tel
Qu'à le servir j'ai passé tout mon temps,
Et je n'en ai pas reçu la valeur d'un œuf
sans coquille. »

XVII

Et Guillaume ajoute : « Messire Bertrand,
cher neveu,
J'ai employé mon temps à servir le roi
430 Et je l'ai vigoureusement élevé en dignité
et en puissance ;
Maintenant il m'a proposé le quart de la France
Exactement comme on ferait un reproche.
En échange de mes services il veut me donner
un salaire !

Mais par l'apôtre que l'on va prier à Rome,
Je songe à lui arracher la couronne de la tête :
Je la lui ai mis et je veux la lui ôter*. »
Bertrand réplique : « Seigneur, vous ne parlez
                        pas en baron.
Vous ne devez pas menacer votre légitime
                        seigneur,
Mais vous devez l'élever en dignité et en
                        puissance,
440   Le secourir et lui venir en aide contre tous
                        les hommes. »
Le comte répond : « Vous dites vrai, cher
                        neveu ;
On doit toujours aimer la loyauté.
Dieu l'ordonne, lui qui doit juger toute chose. »

XVIII

« Oncle Guillaume, propose le sage Bertrand,
Allons donc parler maintenant à Louis,
Vous et moi, dans ce vaste palais,
Pour solliciter un don auquel je viens de penser.
— De quoi s'agirait-il ? » demande Guil-
                        laume le vaillant.
Et Bertrand répond : « Je vais vous parler
                        franchement.
450   Demandez-lui le pays d'Espagne,
Tortolouse et Portpaillart-sur-mer,
Puis Nîmes, la puissante cité,

Et encore Orange qui mérite tant d'être louée*.
S'il vous l'accorde*, cela n'implique aucune
reconnaissance,
Car jamais il n'y a commandé de troupes
Ni enrôlé de chevaliers ;
Il peut bien vous donner ce domaine,
Son royaume n'en souffrira guère. »
A ces mots, Guillaume a éclaté de rire :
460 « Mon neveu, dit-il, heureuse, l'heure de
ta naissance !
J'y avais bien pensé aussi,
Mais je voulais auparavant t'en parler. »
Se prenant par la main, ils sont remontés
au palais,
Pour ne s'arrêter qu'à la salle du trône.
A leur vue, le roi s'est levé pour venir à leur
rencontre ;
Puis il dit à Guillaume : « Asseyez-vous donc.
— C'est inutile, Sire, répond le comte bien né,
Je voudrais seulement vous dire un mot
Et vous demander un don auquel je viens de
songer. »
470 Le roi s'exclame : « Bénédiction de Dieu !
Si vous voulez château, cité,
Bourg ou ville, donjon ou place forte,
Je vous l'accorde très volontiers.
Si vous voulez prendre la moitié de mon
royaume,
Je vous la donne, seigneur, et de plein gré,

Car vous avez toujours été d'une grande fidélité
à mon égard
Et c'est grâce à vous que j'ai été proclamé
roi de France. »
A ces mots, Guillaume éclate de rire ;
Sans plus attendre, il s'adresse au roi en ces
termes :
480   « Je ne vous demanderai jamais un tel
don,
Mais je sollicite le pays d'Espagne,
Tortolouse et Portpaillart-sur-mer,
Je sollicite la cité de Nîmes,
Orange enfin qui mérite tant d'être louée.
Si vous m'accordez ce domaine, cela n'impli-
que aucune reconnaissance,
Car jamais vous n'y avez commandé de troupes
Ni pris en charge de chevaliers,
Et vous n'appauvrirez pas votre patrimoine. »
A ces mots, le roi éclate de rire.

XIX

490   « Seigneur Louis, dit Guillaume le fort,
Pour Dieu ! donne-moi tous les cols d'Espagne :
Dès que la terre sera mienne, ses trésors
t'appartiendront ;
Mille chevaliers viendront de là pour agrandir
ton armée.

XX

« Roi, donne-moi Valsure la grande,
Et avec elle, Nîmes et sa solide fortification.
J'en délogerai le vil païen Otrant
Qui a anéanti tant de Français, sans motif,
Et qui en a chassé de tant de domaines.
Si Dieu veut m'accorder son aide, par sa
volonté,
500 Je ne vous demande pas d'autre terre,
Sire. »

XXI

« Donnez-moi, Sire, Valsore et Valsure,
Donnez-moi Nîmes avec ses hautes tours
pointues,
Puis Orange, la cité redoutable,
Et le pays de Nîmes avec tous ses pâturages,
Près des ravins où le Rhône a son cours*. »
Louis s'écrie : « Seigneur Dieu, aidez-moi !
Ce domaine sera-t-il gardé par un seul
homme ? »
Mais Guillaume répond : « Je ne me soucie pas
de me reposer.
Je chevaucherai le soir et au clair de lune,
510 Revêtu du rembourrage* de mon haubert,
Et j'en délogerai la mauvaise engeance sarra-
sine. »

XXII

« Seigneur Guillaume, dit le roi, écoutez-moi.

Au nom de l'apôtre que l'on va prier au
Parc de Néron,

Cette terre n'est pas à moi, je ne peux vous
la donner ;

Ce sont les Sarrasins et les Esclers qui la
possèdent :

Clareau d'Orange et son frère Aceré,

Golias et le roi Desramé,

Arrogant, Mirant et Barré,

Quinzepaumes et son frère Gondré,

520 Otrant de Nîmes et le roi Murgalé.

Le roi Thibaut doit y être couronné* ;

Il a épousé Orable, la sœur de l'émir :

C'est la plus belle femme que l'on puisse
rencontrer

En pays païen ou chrétien.

Je crains bien que, si vous vous jetez au
milieu d'eux,

Vous ne puissiez libérer cette terre.

Je vous en prie, restez plutôt dans la mienne ;

Faisons deux parts égales de nos villes :

Vous aurez Chartres et vous me laisserez
Orléans

530 Ainsi que la couronne, car je n'en souhaite
pas plus.

— Je n'en ferai rien, Sire, répond Guillaume
                                    le vaillant,
Car vos loyaux barons diraient bientôt :
« Regardez Guillaume, le marquis au court nez,
Comme il a rehaussé son seigneur légitime :
Le roi lui a donné la moitié de son royaume,
Et il ne lui en paie pas un denier de rente.
Il lui a bien rogné ses revenus ! »

XXIII

« Seigneur Guillaume, noble guerrier, dit le roi,
Que vous importent de méchants reproches ?
Je ne veux pas que vous me laissiez seul
                              dans mon domaine.
Vous aurez Chartres et vous me laissez Orléans
Ainsi que la couronne, je ne vous en demande
                                    pas plus.
— Je n'en ferai rien, Sire, riposte Guillaume,
Pas pour tout l'or du monde.
Je me refuse à vous ôter une part de votre
                              domaine ;
Au contraire, je l'accroîtrai par le fer et
                              par l'acier.
Vous êtes mon seigneur et je ne veux pas
                        vous porter tort*.
(Ne savez-vous pas pourquoi je dois vous
                                    quitter ?)
C'était au moment de la saint Michel :

540

Je suis allé à Saint-Gilles et revenu par Montpellier*

550   Où un noble chevalier* m'offrit l'hospita-
lité ;

Il me donna abondamment à boire et à manger,

Ainsi que du foin et de l'avoine pour mon
fougueux coursier.

Quand nous eûmes terminé notre repas,

Il alla se divertir dans la prairie

Avec ses gens, le courtois chevalier*.

(Je voulais reprendre ma route)

Quand sa femme saisit les rênes de ma mon-
ture ;

Je descendis de cheval tandis qu'elle me
tenait l'étrier.

Puis elle me fit monter à un étage supérieur
de la maison,

Et ensuite à une pièce encore plus haute* ;

560   Tout d'un coup, elle se jeta à mes pieds.

Je pensai, cher seigneur, qu'elle me « requérait
d'amour »

Ou de ce qu'une femme demande à un homme.

Si j'en avais été sûr, je ne me serais pas appro-
ché d'elle,

Fusse pour un don de mille livres* !

Je lui demandai : « Madame, femme, que
voulez-vous ?

— Pitié, Guillaume, très noble chevalier,

Prenez cette terre en compassion,

Pour l'amour de Dieu qui fut mis en croix ! »
Elle me fit regarder par la fenêtre :
570 Je vis tout le pays rempli de démons
Qui brûlaient les villes, violaient les couvents,
Détruisaient les chapelles, renversaient les
clochers,
Tordaient les seins des femmes nobles,
Si bien que mon cœur fut rempli de pitié.
Je promis à Dieu qui est au ciel dans sa gloire
Et à saint Gilles que je revenais de prier
De porter secours aux gens de ce pays
Avec autant de troupes que j'en pourrais
commander. »

XXIV

580 « Seigneur Guillaume, dit Louis le noble,
Puisque la terre que je vous offre ne vous
plaît pas,
Aussi vrai que je demande l'aide de Dieu,
j'en suis triste et j'en souffre.
Noble chevalier, approchez-vous ;
Je vais accéder, vraiment, à votre désir.
Recevez l'Espagne en fief, soyez-en investi
par ce gant ;
Je vous la donne selon l'accord suivant :
Si vous éprouvez de la peine ou de la difficulté,
Ni ici ni ailleurs je ne pourrai vous aider. »
Guillaume répond : « Je ne demande rien
de plus

590   Qu'un seul secours en sept ans. »
        Louis ajoute : « Je vous l'accorde avec joie.
        Je vais agir, vraiment, selon votre volonté.
        — Merci beaucoup, Sire, dit le comte, main-
                                tenant attention ! »
        Le comte Guillaume a regardé alors autour
                                de lui.
        Il a avisé Guielin et Bertrand
        Qui étaient ses neveux, et fils de Bernard de
                                Brébant.
        Il les interpelle à haute voix et tout le monde
                                l'entend :
        « Avancez-vous, Guielin et Bertrand.
        Vous êtes mes amis et mes proches parents ;
600   Présentez-vous devant le roi :
        Pour ce fief que je sollicite ici,
        Recevez le gant tous les deux avec moi ;
        Vous partagerez avec moi peines et profits. »
        A ces mots, Guielin sourit d'un air rusé
        Et dit tout bas si bien qu'on ne l'entend pas :
        « Je vais faire beaucoup de chagrin à mon
                                oncle.

        — N'agis pas ainsi, mon frère, lui dit le
                                comte Bertrand,
        Car le puissant Guillaume est très farouche.
        — Et que m'importe ? répond le jeune Guielin,
610   Je suis trop jeune, je n'ai que vingt ans ;
        Je ne peux pas encore supporter une si grande
                                fatigue. »

Son père, Bernard de Brébant, l'a entendu :
Peu s'en faut qu'il ne devienne fou.
Il lève la main et le frappe durement :
« Ah ! fou perfide, tu viens de me causer
                              du chagrin ;
Je vais te mettre en présence du roi.
Par l'apôtre que prient les pénitents,
Si tu ne reçois pas le gant avec Guillaume,
Je te donnerai un grand coup de cette épée
620 Et il n'y aura pas de médecin à partir d'au-
                              jourd'hui
    Pour te soigner désormais durant toute ton
                              existence.
Gagne un fief puisque tu n'en possèdes pas,
Comme je l'ai fait quand j'étais jeune ;
Car, par l'apôtre que prient les pénitents,
Tu n'auras jamais du mien la valeur d'un gant,
Mais je le donnerai entièrement selon mon
                              désir. »
Guielin et Bertrand s'avancèrent.
Ils montèrent debout sur une table
Et s'écrièrent à voix haute et claire :
630 « Messire Bernard de Brébant nous a bat-
                              tus* ;
Mais, par l'apôtre que prient les pénitents,
Les Sarrasins et les Persans nous paieront cela.
Ils peuvent dire qu'ils sont entrés dans une
                              année néfaste :
C'est par centaines et par milliers qu'ils
                              mourront. »

XXV

Guillaume est monté sur une table
Et s'est mis à crier de sa voix claire :
« Écoutez-moi, barons de France.
Aussi vrai que je demande l'aide de Dieu,
                                    je peux me vanter
D'avoir plus de terre que trente de mes pairs
                                    réunis,
640   Mais je n'en ai pas encore libéré un jour-
                                    nal*.

Je le dis aux jeunes gens pauvres
Qui ont des roussins éclopés et des vêtements
                                    déchirés,
Et qui ont servi sans rien conquérir ;
S'ils veulent, en ma compagnie, faire leurs
                                    preuves à la bataille,
Je leur donnerai argent, domaines,
Châteaux, terres, donjons, forteresses,
Pourvu qu'ils m'aident à conquérir le pays,
A exalter et à glorifier la loi divine*.
Voilà ce que je veux dire aux jeunes gens
                                    pauvres,
650   Aux écuyers qui ont des vêtements usés :
S'ils viennent avec moi conquérir l'Espagne,
M'aident à libérer le pays,
A exalter et à glorifier la loi divine,

Je leur donnerai en abondance deniers, argent
                                       brillant,
Châteaux, terres, donjons, forteresses,
Destriers d'Espagne, et ils seront armés cheva-
                                         liers. »

XXVI

A ces paroles, ils sont joyeux et contents* ;
Ils se mettent à crier à voix très haute :
« Seigneur Guillaume, pour Dieu, ne tardez
                                          pas.
660 Celui qui est sans cheval ira à pied avec
                                        vous. »
Il fallait voir les écuyers pauvres,
Et avec eux les chevaliers pauvres !
Ils rejoignent Guillaume, le marquis au fier
                                       visage.
En peu de temps il réunit trente mille hommes,
Équipés d'armes selon leurs possibilités,
Qui tous ont promis et juré
De ne pas lui faire défaut même si on devait
                          leur couper les membres.
A la vue de cette armée, le comte est joyeux
                                  et content ;
Il leur dit merci au nom du Dieu de gloire.
670 Le comte Guillaume s'est comporté sage-
                                        ment ;
Il va prendre congé de Louis ;

4

Le roi le lui donne de grand gré :
« Allez, cher seigneur, au nom du Dieu
glorieux du ciel !
Que Jésus dans sa gloire vous accorde de
bien réussir
Et de revenir sain et sauf ! »
Guillaume se retire, le marquis au fier visage,
Et avec lui, de nombreux chevaliers nobles.
Au milieu de la salle, voici qu'arrive le vieil
Aymon ;
Que Dieu l'anéantisse, le glorieux roi du ciel !
680   Sans plus attendre, Aymon s'adresse à
Louis :
« Juste empereur, comme vous êtes joué !
— Comment cela, cher seigneur ? demande
Louis.
— Sire, répond Aymon, je vais vous l'appren-
dre clairement :
Maintenant, Guillaume le guerrier part,
Et de nombreux chevaliers nobles l'accom-
pagnent.
Il vous a ainsi privé de la fine fleur de France ;
S'il vous naît une guerre, vous ne pourrez
vous tirer d'affaire.
Et je crois bien que Guillaume reviendra
à pied ;
Tous les autres seront réduits à mendier. »
690   — Vous ne parlez pas raisonnablement, répond
Louis.

Guillaume le guerrier est très preux ;
Nulle part n'existe un meilleur chevalier.
Il m'a bien servi par le fer et par l'acier.
Que Jésus plein de gloire lui accorde un bon
                                              retour
Et aussi la libération de toute l'Espagne. »
Il y avait là un noble chevalier
Qu'on appelait Gautier le Tolosant.
Quand il entendit calomnier Guillaume,
Il fut très peiné et plein de courroux.
700 Rapidement il descend de la salle,
Rejoint Guillaume, le retient par l'étrier
Et les rênes de son vif destrier :
« Seigneur, dit-il, vous êtes un excellent
                                          chevalier,
Mais au palais vous ne valez pas un denier.
— Qui donc prétend cela ? demande Guillaume
                                        le terrible.
— Seigneur, répond Gautier, je ne dois pas
                                  vous le cacher :
Par la foi que je vous dois, il s'agit du vieil
                                          Aymon ;
Il s'efforce de vous desservir auprès du roi. »
Guillaume dit : « Il le paiera cher.
710 Si Dieu m'accorde de pouvoir revenir,
Je lui ferai couper tous les membres
Ou je le ferai pendre au gibet ou noyer. »
Mais Gautier réplique : « Je ne me soucie
                                  pas de menacer :

L'homme qui menace ne vaut pas un denier ;
Aussi voudrais-je vous prier de faire ceci :
Récompensez-le selon son service.

C'est ici que vous devez commencer la guerre ;
Aymon est le premier à avoir contesté votre
expédition. »

Guillaume répond : « Vous dites vrai, sur
ma tête ! »

720   Le baron descend de cheval et Gautier lui
tient l'étrier ;

Côte à côte ils gravissent l'escalier.

A leur vue, le roi se dresse pour aller à leur
rencontre,

Entoure de ses deux bras le cou de Guillaume

Et lui donne trois baisers avec une très grande
tendresse.

Très doucement il lui a adressé la parole :

« Seigneur Guillaume, y a-t-il quelque chose
qui vous plaise

Et que je puisse vous procurer* à prix d'or
ou d'argent ?

Vous l'aurez sans limite selon votre désir.

— Merci beaucoup, Sire, a répondu Guillaume.

730   J'ai tout ce dont j'ai besoin ;

Mais je voudrais vous adresser la prière
suivante :

Ne choisissez plus un coquin comme conseil-
ler. »

Alors messire Guillaume regarde derrière lui ;
Au milieu de la salle, il aperçoit le vieil Aymon.
Dès qu'il le voit, il se met à l'insulter :
« Hé ! canaille, coquin, que Dieu t'anéantisse !
Pourquoi te mêles-tu de juger un homme loyal
Quand durant ma vie je ne t'ai nui en rien ?
Pourquoi te mêles-tu de tant me dénigrer ?
740   Par saint Denis que l'on va prier,
Avant que tu ne sortes, je pense te le faire
                                    payer cher. »
Il s'avance après avoir retroussé ses manches ;
Du poing gauche, il saisit Aymon par les
                                    cheveux,
Lève le poing droit, le frappe dans le cou,
Lui brise la nuque par le milieu,
Et l'abat mort à ses pieds.
Puis le comte Guillaume le prend par la tête,
Gautier le Tolosant, par les jambes,
Et ils le jettent par la fenêtre, dans le jardin,
750   Sur un pommier, si bien qu'ils lui ont rompu
                                    les os.
« Dehors, font-ils, coquin, voyou,
Le mensonge ne te rapportera plus un denier !
— Seigneur Louis, ajoute Guillaume le terri-
                                    ble,
Ne faites plus confiance à une canaille ou
                                    à un menteur
Car votre père n'eut jamais d'estime pour
                                    aucun.

Je vais partir à l'aventure pour l'Espagne ;
La terre sera à vous, Sire, si je la conquiers.
— Allez, cher seigneur, à la grâce de Dieu,
le Seigneur du ciel,
Que Jésus dans sa gloire vous accorde de
bien réussir,
760   Et que je vous revoie sain, sauf et intact ! »

L'expédition

Guillaume part, le marquis au fier visage.
En sa compagnie se trouvent de nombreux
                    et puissants personnages,
Et aussi Guielin et messire Bertrand ses neveux.
Ils emmènent avec eux trois cents chevaux
                    de bât.
Je vais vous dire ce que portent les premiers :
Calices d'or, missels et psautiers,
Chapes de soie, croix et encensoirs ;
Quand les Français seront dans le royaume
                    ravagé,
Ils serviront tous le Seigneur Dieu en premier.

XXVII

770   Je vais vous dire ce que portent les
                    suivants :
Vases d'or pur, missels et bréviaires,
Crucifix et très riches nappes d'autel ;

Quand les Français seront dans le royaume
sauvage,
Ils serviront Jésus, l'esprit pur.

XXVIII

Je vais vous dire ce que porte le dernier tiers :
Pots, poêles, chaudrons et trépieds,
Crocs aigus, tenailles et landiers ;
Quand ils viendront dans le royaume ravagé,
Ils pourront ainsi préparer une bonne nourri-
ture ;
780   Ils serviront Guillaume le guerrier,
Et ensuite, tous ses chevaliers.

XXIX

Guillaume part avec sa noble compagnie ;
Il recommande à Dieu la France et Aix-la-
Chapelle,
Paris, Chartres et tout le reste du pays.
Ils traversent la Bourgogne, le Berry et
l'Auvergne* ;
Ils arrivent un soir au pied des cols,
Ils y dressent tentes, pavillons et installent
leurs quartiers.

XXX

Après avoir allumé les feux des cuisines,

Les cuisiniers se hâtent de préparer le repas.
790 Le comte Guillaume est sous sa tente ;
Il se met à pousser de profonds soupirs,
Il se plonge dans de graves songeries*.
Survient Bertrand qui le regarde :
« Mon oncle, dit-il, pourquoi vous désolez-
vous ?
Êtes-vous une dame pleurant sur son veuvage ?
— Que non, vraiment, mon neveu, mais je
pense à autre chose ;
A ce que diront maintenant les nobles cheva-
liers :
« Voyez Guillaume, le marquis au fier visage,
Comme il a traité son seigneur naturel :
800 Ce dernier voulait lui donner la moitié de
son royaume ;
Il se montra si insensé qu'il ne lui en sut
aucun gré
Mais prit l'Espagne sur laquelle il n'avait
aucun droit légitime. »
Je ne pourrai plus voir quatre personnes
assemblées
Sans me figurer qu'elles parlent de moi.
— Mon oncle Guillaume, laissez cela,
Ne vous mettez pas en colère pour un tel
sujet :
Notre avenir dépend entièrement du Seigneur
Dieu ;
Demandez l'eau et allons souper.

— Mon neveu, dit le comte, j'y consens
volontiers. »

810 Ils font demander l'eau à son de trompe,

Puis ils s'asseoient ensemble pour souper ;

Ils ont mangé à satiété de la venaison de
sanglier,

Des grues, des oies sauvages et des paons
épicés.

Puis quand ils sont pleinement rassasiés,

Les écuyers viennent retirer les nappes.

Les chevaliers regagnent leurs quartiers ;

Dès le lendemain au lever du jour,

Ils montent sur leurs rapides destriers

Et vont questionner le marquis Guillaume :

820 « Seigneur, demandent-ils, quels sont vos
projets ?

Dites-nous en quel endroit vous voulez aller.

— Nobles chevaliers, vous êtes tous inquiets ;

Il n'y a pas encore longtemps que nous avons
quitté notre demeure.

Nous irons directement à Brioude au tombeau
du saint qui y est honoré,

Ensuite à Notre-Dame du Puy :

Là nous lui offrirons une partie de nos biens,

Et elle priera pour la chrétienté. »

Ils répondent : « Nous sommes à vos ordres. »

Alors ils chevauchèrent en rangs serrés,

830 Et ils franchirent les collines et les mon-
tagnes.

XXXI

Suivant les directives que leur donne Guil-
laume,
Ils traversent le Berry et l'Auvergne,
Laissant Clermont et Montferrand à main
droite.
Ils évitent la ville et ses opulentes demeures,
Car ils ne veulent faire aucun mal aux gens
du bourg.

XXXII

Ils couchèrent près de là pendant la nuit
et s'en allèrent au matin,
Après avoir ôté les tentes, plié les pavillons
Et chargé le tout sur les chevaux de bât*.
Ils chevauchèrent à travers bois et forêts,
840   Suivirent la voie Regordane*,
Et ne s'arrêtèrent pas avant Le Puy.

XXXIII

Le comte Guillaume va prier à l'église ;
Il a posé trois marcs d'argent sur l'autel,
Quatre pièces de soie et trois tapis ornés
de rosaces*.

Elle est somptueuse, l'offrande que les nobles
ont faite,

Ni avant ni après il n'y en eut de semblable.

Guillaume au court nez sort de l'église ;

Aussitôt il harangue ses compagnons :

« Barons, dit-il, prêtez-moi attention.

850   Voici les terres de la race criminelle ;

Désormais vous ne pourrez aller en avant

Sans que chaque homme que vous rencon-
trerez

Ne soit un Sarrasin ou un Escler.

Prenez vos armes, montez à cheval,

Allez au fourrage, chevaliers loyaux et renom-
més.

Si Dieu vous aide, profitez-en ;

Que tout le pays soit à votre disposition. »

Ils répondent : « Nous sommes à vos ordres. »

Ils revêtent leurs hauberts, lacent leurs heaumes ornés de pierreries,

860   Ceignent leurs épées au pommeau d'or niel-
lé,

Montent sur leurs chevaux rapides ;

Ils pendent à leurs cous leurs solides boucliers
bossués au centre

Et tiennent en leurs poings leurs épieux niellés.

Ils sortent de la ville en rangs serrés,

Et font porter l'oriflamme devant eux.

Ils s'acheminent directement vers Nîmes.

Combien de heaumes vit-on étinceler alors !

A l'avant-garde se trouvaient le fameux Bertrand,

Gautier de Termes, Gilemer l'Escot

870   Et Guielin, preux et pourvu de bon sens*.

Guillaume le vaillant formait l'arrière-garde

Avec dix mille Français bien armés

Qui étaient prêts à la bataille.

Ils n'avaient pas parcouru quatre lieues

Qu'ils rencontrèrent sur leur route un vilain ;

Il vient de Saint-Gilles où il a séjourné,

Avec quatre bœufs qu'il a achetés

Et trois enfants dont il est le père.

Le vilain pense sagement

880   Que le sel est cher dans son pays natal ;

Il a dressé un tonneau sur son chariot

Et il l'a rempli de sel à ras bord.

Les trois enfants dont il est le père

Jouent, rient et sont bien pourvus de pain ;

Ils jouent à la billette* sur le sel.

Les Français rient ; que pourraient-ils faire d'autre ?

Le comte Bertrand interpelle le vilain :

« Dis-nous, vilain, au nom de ta religion, où es-tu né ? »

Il répond : « Vous saurez la vérité.

890   Par Mahomet, seigneur, je suis de Laval-sur-Cler.

Je viens de Saint-Gilles où j'ai fait des achats.

Maintenant je retourne chez moi pour engran-
ger mon blé :
Si Mahomet voulait me le préserver,
J'en serais bien approvisionné, tant j'en ai
semé. »
Les Français lui répondent : « Tu as parlé
comme un sot !
Puisque tu crois que Mahomet est Dieu
Et que grâce à lui tu peux avoir richesse
et abondance,
Froid en hiver ou chaleur en été,
On devrait te couper tous les membres*. »
900   Guillaume intervient : « Barons, laissez
cela.
Je voudrais lui parler d'une autre affaire. »

XXXIV

Le comte Guillaume se met à lui parler ainsi :
« Dis-moi, vilain, au nom de la religion
que tu observes,
Es-tu allé à Nîmes, la cité puissante et bien
pourvue ?
— Oui vraiment, seigneur, ils m'ont réclamé
le péage ;
Je suis très pauvre et je n'ai pu le donner ;
Ils me laissèrent quand ils virent mes enfants.
— Parle-moi, vilain, de l'état de la ville. »

L'autre répond : « Je peux très bien vous
                                    renseigner.
910   Nous y avons vu vendre deux gros pains
                                pour un denier ;
On peut acheter ici, avec un denier, deux fois
                            plus qu'ailleurs ;
La vie y est bon marché si la situation n'a pas
                                        empiré.
— Idiot, dit Guillaume, ce n'est pas ce que
                            je te demande,
Il s'agit des chevaliers païens de la ville,
Du roi Otrant et de ses compagnons. »
Le vilain répond : « A ce sujet j'ignore tout,
Et je me garderai bien de mentir. »
Il y avait là Garnier, un noble chevalier ;
C'était un vavasseur* qui s'y connaissait
                                      en ruse
920   Et était fécond en ressources ingénieuses.
Il regarda les quatre bœufs qui s'avançaient :
« Seigneur, fait-il, Dieu me bénisse !
L'homme qui posséderait mille tonneaux sem-
                                      blables
A celui qui est posé sur ce chariot,
Tous remplis de chevaliers,
Et les conduirait à Nîmes,
Pourrait de cette façon prendre la ville. »
Guillaume s'écrie : « Sur ma tête, vous dites
                                        vrai.
Je vais le faire si mes barons l'approuvent. »

XXXV

930   Suivant l'avis donné par Garnier,
Ils font faire halte au vilain
Et lui apportent un copieux repas
Accompagné de pain, de vin, de boisson
pimentée et de claret.
Il mange avec ses enfants car ils avaient très
faim.
Une fois le vilain bien rassasié,
Le comte Guillaume convoque ses barons
Et ils se rassemblent sans retard.
Aussitôt il les harangue :
« Barons, dit-il, écoutez-moi bien.
940   L'homme qui aurait mille tonneaux percés
de trous d'air*,
Semblables à celui que vous voyez sur ce
chariot,
Emplis de chevaliers armés,
Et qui les conduirait sur la grand'route*
Tout droit à Nîmes, la puissante cité,
Pourrait y pénétrer ainsi,
Sans coup férir. »
Ils répliquent : « Vous avez raison.
Seigneur Guillaume, noble chevalier, occupez-
vous-en donc.
En ce pays il y a des quantités de voitures ;

950   On y trouve chars et charrettes.
      Faites retourner votre armée
      Par la voie Regordane où nous sommes passés,
      Et faites prendre les bœufs par la force. »
      Guillaume reprend : « C'est bien raisonné. »

XXXVI

Suivant l'avis de son baron,
Le comte Guillaume a fait retourner ses
                                    hommes
Par la voie Regordane, à quatorze lieues
                              en arrière.
Ils s'emparent des chariots, des bœufs et
                              des tonneaux.
Les bons vilains, après avoir fabriqué et
                        assemblé les tonneaux,
960   Les assujettissent sur les chariots et doublent
                              les attelages*.
Qu'importe à Bertrand si les vilains pro-
                                    testent :
Quiconque a maugréé s'en est bien repenti,
Car il a perdu la vue et a été pendu par la
                                    gorge.

XXXVII

Qui aurait vu les rudes vilains aller et venir
Et porter doloires et cognées,

Lier les tonneaux, tout remettre à neuf,
Cheviller et munir de barres chariots et
charrettes,
Qui aurait vu les chevaliers entrer dans
les tonneaux,
Aurait gardé le souvenir d'un grand exploit.
970   Chacun se munit d'un gros maillet ;
Quand ils arriveront à la ville de Nîmes
Et qu'ils entendront sonner le cor de leur chef,
Nos Français pourront employer toutes leurs
forces.

XXXVIII

Dans d'autres tonneaux sont placées les lances,
Et sur chacun les Français ont fait deux
marques ;
Ainsi quand ils arriveront chez la race cruelle,
Les soldats de France ne seront pas en péril*.

XXXIX

Dans d'autres tonneaux encore ont été placés
les boucliers,
Et sur chaque fond ils ont tracé deux signes* ;
980   Ainsi quand ils arriveront chez les Sarrasins,
Nos Français ne seront pas en péril.

XL

Le comte se hâte d'apprêter le charroi.
Qui aurait vu les vilains du pays
Lier les tonneaux, les réparer et les munir
                              de fonds,
Retourner et renverser les grands chariots,
Qui aurait vu les chevaliers entrer dans les
                              tonneaux,
Aurait gardé le souvenir d'un grand exploit*.
Maintenant nous devons chanter messire Ber-
                              trand
Et dire comment il s'est accoutré :
990   Il mit une cotte de bure sombre
Et se chaussa de souliers extraordinaires :
Énormes, en cuir de bœuf, avec le dessus percé.
« Dieu, dit Bertrand, grand roi de majesté,
Ils m'auront bientôt tout meurtri les pieds. »
En l'entendant, Guillaume a éclaté de rire.
« Mon neveu, dit le comte, écoutez-moi bien.
Faites avancer ces bœufs dans le vallon. »
Et Bertrand répond : « Vous parlez pour
                              ne rien dire.
Je ne sais pas manier l'aiguillon
000   Pour mettre des bœufs en marche. »
En l'entendant, Guillaume a encore éclaté
                              de rire.

Mais il est arrivé une fâcheuse aventure à
Bertrand

Car il ne s'y connaissait pas du tout dans
ce métier !

Avant qu'il comprenne ce qui se passe,
le voilà entré dans une fondrière ;

Le chariot s'y est enfoncé jusqu'aux moyeux ;

A cette vue, Bertrand manque devenir enragé.

Qui l'aurait vu aller dans la fange

Et soulever la roue à l'aide de ses épaules

Aurait pu le considérer avec un grand étonne-
ment ;

1010   Il en eut la bouche et le nez meurtris.

En le voyant, Guillaume se mit à railler :

« Cher neveu, dit-il, écoutez-moi.

Vous vous êtes engagé maintenant dans une
tâche

A laquelle il semble bien que vous n'entendez
rien. »

A ces paroles, Bertrand manque devenir fou.

Dans la tonne que le comte Bertrand avait
à conduire

Se trouvaient le baron Gilbert de Falaise,

Gautier de Termes et Gilemer l'Escot :

« Seigneur Bertrand, disent-ils, efforcez-vous
de bien conduire,

1020   Nous nous attendons à tout moment à ce
que vous nous versiez. »

Bertrand leur répond : « Cela viendra en
son temps. »

Maintenant nous chanterons les chevaliers
conducteurs de chariots
Qui devaient aussi mener le charroi :
Ils portent des équipements, des sacoches
et des ceintures,
Ils portent aussi de larges bourses pour
changer la monnaie,
Et montent des mulets et des bêtes de somme
mal en point.
Si vous les aviez vus cheminer tout le long
de la route,
Vous les auriez pris pour des gens de peu.
Dans ce pays ils ne pourront s'avancer,
030   Pour peu qu'il fasse jour et qu'on puisse
les voir,
Sans qu'on les prenne pour des marchands.
Ils passent le Gardon à gué sur la chaussée ;
Ils campent dans une prairie sur l'autre rive.
Maintenant nous allons chanter Guillaume ;
Voyons comment il s'est accoutré.

XLI

Le comte Guillaume revêt une longue tunique
Faite de la bure qu'on trouve dans la région,
Il met de grandes chausses violâtres*,
Des souliers en cuir de bœuf qui serrent
ses chausses ;
040   Il se fixe à la taille la ceinture d'un bourgeois
du pays,

Un couteau dans une belle gaine y pend ;
Il chevauche une jument sans force ;
Deux vieux étriers pendent à sa selle ;
Ses éperons ne datent pas d'hier :
Ils ont bien trente ans d'existence ;
En guise de coiffure, le comte porte un chapeau
de feutre.

XLII

Au bord du Gardon, le long de la rive,
Ils laissent deux mille hommes en armes
De la maison de Guillaume Fierebrace.
1050 Ils éloignent tous les vilains
Pour qu'aucun d'eux n'aille révéler
Quelle marchandise ils comptent sortir des
tonneaux.
Plus de deux mille chevaliers préparent leurs
aiguillons,
Taillent et frappent, et ils s'engagent sur la
route.
D'une seule traite ils arrivent à Nozières,
Puis à Lavardi* d'où fut extraite la pierre
Qui servit à édifier les tours de Nîmes.
Les gens de la ville vaquent à leurs affaires ;
Ils regardent et se disent les uns aux autres :
1060 « Voici venir une grande foule de mar-
chands.
— Vraiment, je n'en ai jamais tant vu. »

Ils pressent leurs chevaux jusqu'au chef des
              marchands,
Et lui demandent : « Quelles marchandises
              transportez-vous ?
— Des étoffes de soie, des draperies pourpres,
              des vêtements de soie,
Des tissus d'écarlate, des tissus verts, bruns,
              de grande valeur*,
Des épieux tranchants, des hauberts et des
              heaumes peints en vert*,
De lourds boucliers et des épées bien affilées. »
Les païens disent : « Il y en a pour de l'argent.
Il faut que vous alliez au péage. »

XLIII

1070 Les Français ont tant chevauché et che-
              miné,
       Franchissant vallées, montagnes et collines,
       Qu'ils sont arrivés à la cité de Nîmes.
       Ils font franchir la porte à leur charroi,
       Une voiture après l'autre, en file serrée.
       La nouvelle s'est répandue à travers la ville :
       « De riches marchands venus d'un autre pays
       Amènent des marchandises comme on n'en
              a jamais vu ;
       Mais ils ont tout enfermé dans des tonneaux. »
       Le roi Otrant, en l'apprenant,
080   Descend les degrés de son palais avec Har-
              pin :

Ils étaient frères, s'aimaient beaucoup,
Et gouvernaient la belle cité.
Ils se sont rendus directement au marché,
Escortés de deux cents païens.

La prise de Nîmes

XLIV

Seigneurs, écoutez, que Dieu vous bénisse*,
Le glorieux, le fils de sainte Marie,
Cette chanson que je vais vous dire :
Elle ne parle ni d'orgueil ni de folie,
Elle n'a pas été inventée par mensonge ;

C'est la chanson des preux qui ont conquis
                      l'Espagne ;
Au nom de Jésus, ils ont exalté la foi chrétienne.
Cette ville de Nîmes dont je chante pour vous
                      l'histoire
Se trouve sur la route* qui mène au sanctuaire
                de Monseigneur saint Gilles*.
(Il y avait dans la ville une place ancienne
Où l'on prie maintenant la Vierge dans une
                      église.)
Mais alors il n'y avait pas d'église,

Car régnait la religion de l'engeance païenne ;
On priait à cet endroit Mahomet et ses idoles
Ainsi que Tervagant qui protégeait les païens ;
Ces derniers y tenaient* leurs tribunaux
et leurs conseils
1100 Et s'y réunissaient de tous les quartiers
de la ville.

XLV

Guillaume se dirige directement vers cette place
Où se trouvait un perron* taillé dans du
marbre vert.
Là, Guillaume Fierebrace descendit de cheval,
Prit sa bourse, en défit les cordons ;
Il en tire une grosse poignée de bons deniers
Et dit à celui qui perçoit l'octroi
Qu'il ne veut pas qu'il leur fasse de mal.
Les païens s'écrient : « N'ayez aucune crainte ;
Il n'y a personne, de si puissante lignée soit-il,
1110 Qui, s'il vous disait des paroles d'orgueil
ou d'insolence,
Ne soit pendu par le cou à un arbre. »

XLVI

Pendant qu'ils conversent et discutent ainsi
Avec le comte Guillaume,
Voici venir Harpin et Otrant

Qui demandent le fameux marchand.
Les païens qui étaient là en badauds répon-
                                    dent :
« Le voilà, c'est ce prudhomme avenant,
Avec ce chapeau et cette grande barbe,
Qui donne ses ordres aux autres marchands. »
120   Le roi Otrant l'interpelle le premier :
« D'où êtes-vous, marchand, mon cher ami ?
— Sire, nous sommes de la puissante Angle-
                                    terre,
De Cantorbéry, une riche cité.
— Êtes-vous marié, marchand, mon cher ami ?
— Oui, ma femme est très gracieuse et j'ai
                        dix-huit enfants.
Tous sont petits, il n'y en a que deux grands :
L'un s'appelle Bègue et l'autre, Sorant ;
Les voilà, si vous ne me croyez pas. »
Il leur désigne à la fois Guielin et Bertrand :
130   C'étaient ses neveux, fils de Bernard de
                                    Brébant.
Les païens, qui se mettent à les observer,
                                    disent :
« Vous avez des enfants qui seraient extra-
                        ordinairement beaux
Si seulement ils savaient s'habiller élégam-
                                    ment ! »
Le roi Otrant lui dit aussitôt :
« Quel est votre nom, marchand, mon cher
                                    ami ?

— Très cher seigneur, Tiacre, en vérité. »
Le païen remarque : « C'est un nom bien laid.
Frère Tiacre, quelle marchandise transportez-
vous ?
— Des étoffes de soie, Sire, du foulard de soie,
des étoffes de lin*,
1140　Des tissus d'écarlate, des tissus verts, violets,
de valeur,
De blancs hauberts, des heaumes solides
et scintillants,
Des épieux tranchants, de lourds boucliers
de qualité,
Des épées brillantes au pommeau d'or étin-
celant*. »
(Le roi dit alors : « Ami, montrez-nous cela. »)
Et Guillaume : « Baron, attendez un peu ;
Les chargements les plus précieux viennent
derrière.
— Qu'est-ce donc qui se trouve là-devant* ?
— De l'encre, du soufre, de l'encens, du vif-
argent,
De l'alun, de la cochenille, du poivre, du safran,
1150　Des peaux de bêtes, de la basane, du cuir
de Cordoue,
Des fourrures de martre, qui sont utiles
en hiver. »
A ces mots, Otrant rit joyeusement,
Et les Sarrasins sont très contents.

XLVII

Le roi Otrant de nouveau l'interpelle :
« Frère Tiacre, au nom de votre religion,
S'il vous plaît, dites-nous la vérité.
A mon avis, vous possédez un grand avoir,
Vous qui le faites amener ici par chariots ;
Faites-nous la grâce de nous en donner,
60 A moi et à ces autres jeunes gens.
Vous y trouverez votre bénéfice, si vous
                    continuez la route. »
Guillaume répond : « Cher seigneur, patientez
                    un peu ;
Je ne quitterai pas cette ville aujourd'hui :
La place est bonne, je veux y rester.
Vous ne verrez pas demain passer midi,
Sonner les vêpres ni le soleil se coucher,
Sans que je vous fasse tant donner de mon bien
Que le plus fort d'entre vous en aura sa
                    charge. »
Les païens disent : « Marchand, tu es bien
                    brave,
70 Mais tu n'es généreux qu'en paroles.
Si tu es honnête homme, nous le saurons bien.
— Je le suis vraiment, dit-il, et plus que vous
                    ne le croyez.
Je n'ai jamais été un trompeur ni un avare ;

Mon bien est à l'entière disposition
Des amis qui sont dans mon intimité. »
Le comte a appelé l'un de ses hommes :
« Dis-moi, tous mes chariots sont-ils entrés ?
— Oui vraiment, seigneur, grâce à Dieu. »
A travers les rues il commence à les diriger ;
1180 Il les fait décharger sur les larges places,
Car il ne veut être gêné par rien,
Afin de pouvoir se dégager, si besoin est.
La porte du palais est si obstruée
Qu'il sera ardu d'y entrer pour les Sarrasins.

XLVIII

Le roi Otrant se met à questionner Guillaume :
« Frère Tiacre, par la religion dans laquelle
tu vis,
Où as-tu acquis de si grandes richesses
Et en quel pays, sur quel domaine vis-tu ? »
Guillaume répond : « Je vais vous le dire :
1190 J'ai acquis la majeure partie de ma fortune
en douce France.
Maintenant je m'en vais en Lombardie,
En Calabre, en Pouille, en Sicile,
En Allemagne puis en Romagne*,
En Toscane et de là en Hongrie ;
Puis je m'en reviens vers la Galice
Qui est en Espagne, une riche contrée,

Puis je vais en Poitou.et de là en Normandie ;
Enfin en Angleterre, en Écosse où je vis :
Je ne m'arrêterai pas jusqu'au Pays de Galles ;
1200   Je mènerai ma caravane tout droit au Crac
                des Chevaliers*,
A une foire très ancienne.
J'ai fait mon change au royaume de Venise. »
Les païens s'écrient : « Tu as parcouru de
                nombreux pays,
Il n'est pas étonnant, vilain, que tu sois riche. »

XLIX

Écoutez, seigneurs, par le Dieu de majesté,
Comment Guillaume fut reconnu ce jour-là.
Le roi Otrant se mit à l'observer
En l'entendant si bien s'exprimer,
Et il remarqua la bosse qu'il avait sur le nez.
1210   Il se souvient alors de Guillaume au court
                nez,
Fils d'Aymeri de Narbonne-sur-mer.
A cette vue, peu s'en faut qu'il ne perde
                la raison ;
Tout son sang se fige dans ses veines,
Le cœur lui manque, il est sur le point de
                s'évanouir.
Il s'adresse à Guillaume noblement,
Et lui tient le discours que vous allez entendre :

« Frère Tiacre, par la religion que vous
                                    observez,
Cette grosse bosse que vous avez sur le nez,
Qui vous l'a faite ? Gardez-vous de le dissi-
                                    muler,
1220   Car je viens de penser à Guillaume au court
                                    nez,
Ce si redoutable fils d'Aymeri ;
Il a tué les membres de ma puissante famille.
Plût à Mahomet* qui est mon protecteur,
A Tervagant et à ses saintes vertus,
Que je le tienne enfermé dans ces murs
Comme vous-même que je vois devant moi :
Par Mahomet, il serait mis à mal,
Pendu haut et court au gibet, en plein vent,
Ou brûlé sur un bûcher ou mis à mort honteu-
                                    sement. »
1230   A ces mots, Guillaume éclate de rire :
« Sire, dit-il, écoutez-moi.
Au sujet de ce que vous me demandez,
Je vais vous répondre très volontiers.
Alors que j'étais jeune, pauvre et garçon,
Je devins un étonnant larron pour voler
Et tromper : je n'avais pas mon pareil.
Je coupais bourses et sacoches bien fixées ;
Les jeunes nobles et les marchands
Que j'avais volés me prirent sur le fait ;
1240   Avec leurs couteaux, ils m'entamèrent le
                                    nez,

Puis ils me laissèrent m'échapper ;
J'ai commencé alors à pratiquer le métier
                que vous voyez.
Grâce à Dieu, j'ai pu acquérir
Tout ce que vous avez sous les yeux. »
Le païen constate : « Vous êtes un vaillant
                homme.
Vous ne serez jamais pendu au gibet. »
Un Sarrasin a quitté la place ;
Ceux qui le connaissent le nomment Barré :
C'est le sénéchal du roi ;
250 Il a l'intention de préparer le repas
Et d'allumer le feu dans la cuisine.
Il trouve la porte du palais si encombrée
Qu'il ne peut y entrer d'aucune façon.
A cette vue, il manque perdre la raison ;
Il jure par Mahomet qu'il va le faire payer cher.
Il vient trouver Harpin et lui raconte tout :
Harpin était le maître de la riche cité
Avec son frère Otrant le mécréant ;
Barré s'adresse à lui avec déférence :
260 « Mon jeune seigneur, écoutez-moi.
Par Mahomet, il nous arrive une fâcheuse
                aventure
Par la faute de ce vilain qui est entré ici.
Il nous a si bien encombré la porte du palais
Que l'on n'en peut ni entrer ni sortir.
Si l'on m'en croyait et que l'on suivît mon avis,

Nous le ferions mettre en fureur.

Voyez les biens qu'il a réunis ici ;

Il n'en veut rien donner ni à vous ni aux autres.

Faites donc, seigneur, tuer tous ces bœufs :

1270   Ils serviront à apprêter le repas à la cui-
                                              sine. »

Harpin réplique : « Apportez-moi un gros
                                       maillet. »

Et l'autre s'empresse : « A vos ordres. »

Le coquin a quitté la place ;

Il est allé lui chercher un maillet de fer ;

Il revient vers Harpin et le lui met dans la main.

Harpin lève le maillet et tue Baillet

Puis Lonel qui était à côté

— C'étaient les deux limoniers du chariot
                                       principal —.

Il les fait écorcher par le valet,

1280   Pour préparer le repas à la cuisine.

Il pensait en rassasier ses Sarrasins,

Mais avant d'en avoir savouré un morceau,

A mon avis, ils le paieront cher,

Car un Français a assisté à la scène.

En la voyant, il en a eu du déplaisir ;

Il vient trouver Guillaume et lui raconte
                                       toute l'affaire ;

Il lui glisse doucement ces paroles à l'oreille,

Sans éveiller l'attention des Sarrasins et des
                                             Esclers :

« Ma foi, seigneur, il vous arrive une fâcheuse
                                      aventure.
1290   Ils viennent de tuer deux bœufs de votre
                                      charroi,
       Les plus beaux de ceux que nous avions
                                      amenés ;
       Ils appartenaient au brave homme que vous
                                      avez rencontré,
       On les avait placés en tête du charroi.
       Vous savez quels sont ceux qui sont entrés
                                      dans la tonne :
       Le comte Gilbert de Falaise-sur-mer,
       Gautier de Termes et Gilemer l'Escot.
       Bertrand, votre neveu, était chargé de les
                                      conduire ;
       Vous les avez mal protégés. »
       A cette nouvelle, Guillaume manque devenir
                                      fou de colère ;
300   Mais il lui répond doucement à voix
                                      basse :
       « Qui a fait cela ? Garde-toi de ne rien me
                                      cacher.
       — Ma foi, cher seigneur, vous auriez tort
                                      de ne pas le croire :
       C'est Harpin, le maudit félon.
       — Mais pourquoi, diable ? Quel mal leur
                                      reprochait-il ?
       — Je ne sais pas, cher seigneur, au nom de
                                      la foi que je dois à Dieu. »

A l'écouter, Guillaume se sent irrité,
Et il dit assez bas pour n'être pas entendu :
« Par saint Denis qui est mon protecteur,
Aujourd'hui même, cet acte sera payé cher. »
1310 Autour de lui se pressent les Sarrasins
Qui le raillent abondamment et lui cherchent
noise :
Le roi Harpin le leur avait ordonné,
Car il voulait susciter une querelle,
Aidé de son frère Agrapart l'Escler.

L

Écoutez, seigneurs, que Dieu vous bénisse !
Comment ils cherchent querelle à Guillaume.
Le roi Harpin* commence :
« Dis-moi, vilain, Mahomet* te maudisse !
Pourquoi les gens de ta maison ne sont-ils
pas vêtus,
1320 Ni toi non plus, de pelisses ?
Vous seriez mieux appréciés. »
Et Guillaume lui répond : « Je ne dépenserai
pas une alise pour cela.
Quand nous serons retournés
Auprès de ma femme qui m'attend impa-
tiemment,
Chargés de grandes richesses,
Alors je vêtirai luxueusement les gens de
ma maison. »

LI

Le roi Harpin lui objecte avec animosité :
« Dis-moi, vilain, que Mahomet te mette
à mal !
Pourquoi portes-tu de si grands souliers en
cuir de vache,
1330 Pourquoi ta tunique et ton équipement sont-ils
si misérables ?
Tu parais vraiment un homme qui ne se
soigne pas. »
Il s'approche et lui tire la barbe,
Peu s'en faut qu'il ne lui en arrache cent poils.
A cette insulte, Guillaume manque devenir
fou de rage.
Il murmure sans que ne l'entende âme qui vive :
« Même si je porte actuellement de grands
souliers en cuir de vache,
Une tunique et un équipement si misérables,
Je ne m'en nomme pas moins Guillaume
Fierebrace,
Fils d'Aymeri de Narbonne le sage,
340 Le noble comte qui a tant de bravoure.
Ce Sarrasin vient de me faire injure ;
Il ne me connaît pas pour m'avoir tiré la barbe :
Il a eu tort de le faire, par l'apôtre saint Jac-
ques. »

LII

Guillaume poursuit tout bas, à la dérobée :
« Même si je porte actuellement des chausses
                              tachées de boue,
Une tunique trop longue et trop large,
Il est vrai aussi que le seigneur Aymeri est
                              mon père,
Aymeri de Narbonne, homme d'une valeur
                              éprouvée.
Je suis Guillaume, moi dont tu as tiré la barbe ;
1350 Tu as eu tort de le faire, par l'apôtre saint
                              Pierre,
Car avant ce soir, tu le paieras cher. »

LIII

Écoutez, seigneurs, que Dieu accroisse votre
                              valeur,
Comment Guillaume a agi.
Quand il sentit qu'on lui arrachait les poils
                              de la moustache,
Alors qu'on avait déjà tué deux bœufs de
                              son charroi,
Croyez bien qu'il fut très irrité ;
S'il ne se venge pas, il deviendra fou.
Guillaume est monté sur un perron ;
A voix haute il se met à crier :

360 « Païens félons, que Dieu vous anéantisse
tous !

Vous m'avez bien tourné en dérision aujour-
d'hui,

En me traitant de marchand et de vilain ;

Mais en vérité, je ne suis pas un marchand,

Je ne m'appelle pas du tout Tiacre* ;

Car par l'apôtre que l'on va prier au Parc
de Néron,

Vous saurez aujourd'hui quelles marchandises
je mène.

Et toi, Harpin, orgueilleux coquin,

Pourquoi m'as-tu tiré la barbe et la mous-
tache ?

Sache-le bien, tu m'as irrité au plus haut point :

370 Je ne souperai ni ne dînerai

Tant que tu ne l'auras pas payé de ta personne. »

Vivement il se dresse,

Du poing gauche il le saisit par les cheveux,

L'attire à lui, le force à s'incliner,

Lève le poing droit qu'il a gros et carré,

Et dans sa fureur, il lui donne un tel coup

Qu'il lui brise la nuque par le milieu,

Et l'étend mort à ses pieds.

A cette vue, les païens sont hors d'eux ;

380 A voix forte, ils se mettent à crier :

« Coquin, traître, vous ne vous en tirerez pas.

Par Mahomet qui est notre protecteur,

Votre corps sera livré au pire supplice,
Pendu ou brûlé, et la cendre jetée au vent.
C'est pour votre malheur que vous avez osé
                              toucher au roi Harpin. »
Sans plus attendre, ils se ruent sur lui.

LIV

Les païens crient : « Marchand, tu as tort.
Pourquoi as-tu tué le roi Harpin ?
C'est un acte dont tu ne retireras aucun profit ;
1390   Tu ne sortiras pas vivant d'ici. »
Devant le duc on pouvait voir maint poing
                              fermé ;
Les païens croyaient qu'il n'y avait pas davan-
                              tage des nôtres.

Le comte Guillaume met un cor à ses lèvres,
Il en sonne trois fois, à notes aiguës et graves :
Quand ils l'entendent, les barons cachés
Dans les tonneaux où ils étaient enfermés,
Saisissent les maillets et font sauter les fonds.
L'épée à la main, ils bondissent hors des
                              tonneaux
Et crient Montjoie ! avec une énergie éton-
                              nante.
1400   Bientôt il y aura des blessés et des morts.
Une fois les vaillants chevaliers sortis des
                              tonneaux,
Ils se répandent en grand nombre dans les rues.

LV

La mêlée fut grande et étonnante,
Et la bataille affreuse et acharnée.
Quand les païens, les traîtres infâmes, virent
Que les Français étaient si farouches et
                                  si hardis au combat,
Ils coururent aux armes, les traîtres infâmes.
Les païens s'équipent tous sans exception,
Dans leurs maisons et dans leurs forteresses :
410 Ils se préparent à se défendre.
Ils sortent de chez eux, le bouclier en avant,
Au son de la trompette, ils vont au ralliement.
Mais voici un vaillant chevalier
De la maison du puissant Guillaume* ;
Il amène leurs fougueux destriers aux Français
Qui les enfourchent sans perdre une minute.
Ils pendent à leurs cous les solides et lourds
                                           boucliers,
Prennent dans leurs mains les forts épieux
                                           tranchants
Et se jettent en avant, de toutes leurs forces,
                                  au milieu des païens.
420 Ils crient Montjoie ! derrière et devant ces
                                           derniers
Qui vendent chèrement leur vie,
Car la ville est peuplée de leur engeance.

Là on pouvait voir, dans une immense mêlée,
En grand nombre, les hampes de lance se briser
                    sur les lourds boucliers,
Les mailles des hauberts à l'algérienne* être
                    mises en pièces,
Les Sarrasins culbuter morts dans leur sang.
Aucun n'échappa à la tuerie,
Tous moururent sur place.
Le sol est tout couvert de sang.
1430   Otrant tourne bride, il n'a cure de s'attar-
                    der.

LVI

La mêlée est étonnante et rude ;
Les combattants frappent de grands coups
                    d'épée et d'épieu.
Otrant s'enfuit, car il a peur de la mort.
Le comte Guillaume est sur ses talons,
Il le saisit au collet.
Puis il lui adresse deux mots à voix haute :
« Sais-tu, Otrant, contre quelle engeance
                    je me fais justicier ?
Contre l'engeance de ceux qui ne puisent
                    pas leur force en Dieu.
Quand je peux les prendre, ils sont voués
                    à la honte ;
1440   Sache-le vraiment, l'heure de ta mort est
                    venue. »

LVII

Guillaume à la mine hardie ajoute :
« Otrant, roi félon, que le Seigneur Dieu
                              te maudisse !
Si tu crois au Fils de sainte Marie,
Sache-le en vérité, ton âme sera sauvée ;
Sinon, je t'en fais le ferme serment,
Tu perdras_ ta tête
Pour Mahomet qui ne vaut pas une alise. »
Otrant répond : « Je n'ai rien à dire là-dessus ;
Je me conduirai selon ce que veut mon cœur.
450 Par Mahomet, je me refuse absolument
A croire en votre Dieu et à trahir ma reli-
                              gion*. »
A ces paroles, Guillaume est presque fou
                              de colère ;
Il le traîne du haut en bas des marches.
Les Français, en voyant Otrant, se mettent
                              à lui parler :

LVIII

Les Français s'écrient : « Otrant, tu n'as
                              qu'un mot à dire
Pour obtenir six jours de sursis*. »
Le comte Guillaume s'écrie avec violence :

« Au diable, qui l'en priera tant ! »
Ils le jettent dehors par l'une des fenêtres* ;
1460   Il était mort avant d'arriver à terre.
Après lui ils en ont jeté dehors cent autres
Qui ont eu les membres et l'échine rompus.

LIX

Maintenant les Français ont libéré la ville,
Ses hautes tours et ses salles dallées.
Ils ont trouvé du vin et du blé en abondance ;
Il faudrait sept ans pour souffrir de la famine,
Et pour que la ville soit prise et mise à mal.
Il pèse à Guillaume que nos Français ne le
                    sachent pas encore,
Les mille barons qui sont restés au camp.
1470   En haut du palais royal il fait sonner du
                    cor,
Et les nôtres qui sont restés en dehors de la
                    ville l'entendent.
Aussitôt ils montèrent à cheval sans perdre
                    de temps
Et se rendirent à Nîmes tout d'une traite.
En arrivant, ils manifestèrent une grande joie,
Ainsi que les vilains qui les accompagnaient
Et qui réclamèrent leurs chariots et leurs
                    bœufs ;
Les Français, dans leur satisfaction, ne leur
                    opposèrent aucun refus,

Aussi les vilains ne perdirent-ils pas la valeur
                                  d'un denier
Qu'elle ne leur fût largement remboursée ;

480   De surcroît ils reçurent de grandes récom-
                                   penses
Puis retournèrent dans leur pays.
Le bruit de la victoire va jusqu'en France :
Le comte Guillaume a libéré la ville de Nîmes.
On en fait le récit à Louis
Qui, après l'avoir écouté, manifeste une très
                               grande joie ;
Il adore Dieu et sa mère Marie.

NOTES

6. Nous traduisons d'après le manuscrit de Boulogne (C) qui porte : *par le charroi mené*, alors que l'édition Perrier est : *par le charroi monté*.

7-10. Allusion à *La Prise d'Orange* ; ces vers sont à mettre au nombre des preuves de l'existence d'une *Prise d'Orange* primitive, antérieure au *Charroi de Nîmes*. Nous n'avons pas traduit *Escler*, car il n'est nullement établi que ce terme désigne les Slaves. Voir cependant à ce sujet le *Manuel pratique d'ancien français* par G. Raynaud de Lage, éd. Picard, Paris, 1968, p. 31.

11. Le combat de Guillaume et du géant sarrasin Corsolt est l'un des ornements du *Couronnement de Louis* ; la description physique du démoniaque Corsolt se place aux vers 504-10 de cette dernière chanson qui précède le *Charroi*.

14. Au Moyen Age, on ne connaissait que deux saisons : l'été et l'hiver ; bien que le récit commence en mai, nous avons préféré garder le mot *esté*. Nous avons isolé par un espacement les vers 1-13 qui constituent le prologue de la chanson de geste.

29. Ce vers, comme le vers 51, est un refrain ; il interrompt le déroulement de l'histoire. Pour cette raison, nous avons isolé ces deux vers dans notre présentation matérielle.

54. On accède à la salle du trône en gravissant un *marbrin degré* et un *planchié* incliné, précise-t-on dans la plus récente édition du *Charroi, Textes et traitement automatique*, sous la direction de G. De Poerck, éd. Mallier, Saint-Aquilin-de-Pacy, 1970, p. 22. Contrairement à l'éd. De Poerck, nous croyons que le *planchié* des vers 55, 700 et 721 désigne la salle du trône.

63. Notre traduction suit le texte des manuscrits C et B (Londres) : *serez escouté* et rattache ce vers à ce qui précède ; l'apostrophe de Guillaume au roi commence par *Looÿs frere*.

65. Selon l'éd. Perrier, Guillaume se vante d'avoir passé son temps à *tastoner* le roi, à priver de leur héritage la veuve et le jeune enfant ! La variante du Manuscrit A4 (Milan) : *Mout te servi non pas de tastonner* offre un sens plus honorable et que nous adoptons. Cependant J.-Ch. Payen, *De la tradition à l'écriture : à propos d'un livre récent*, Le Moyen Age, Nº 3-4, 1969, p. 531, pense que la leçon retenue par Perrier n'est pas si dépourvue de sens, si la phrase est ponctuée d'un point d'ironie.

84. Nous abandonnons le texte de Perrier : *g'en doie trover* pour traduire celui du manuscrit C : *grain en doi trover* qui est plus clair.

94-101. Ces huit vers représentent une allusion aux événements qui sont rapportés dans le *Couronnement* aux vers 1352-1429. En ce qui concerne le vers 95, nous suivons le texte BC : *Ne me tenissent* et nous remplaçons par une virgule le point qui suit le mot *losangier* dans l'éd. Perrier. Entre les vers 100 et 101 nous donnons la traduction d'un vers du manuscrit C : *Si tres grant terre preïsse o la moillier* qui fournit la subordonnée hypothétique complément du vers 101.

113. Nous traduisons *viande* et non *demande* qui est une erreur de lecture du copiste médiéval.

134-147. Ici se place le rappel détaillé du combat singulier livré par Guillaume contre Corsolt et l'explication renouvelée du surnom *au court nez ;* on consultera pour le commentaire de ce passage J. Frappier, *Les chansons de geste du cycle de Guillaume d'Orange*, éd. SEDES, Paris, 1967, II, p. 205-7.

141-144. J. Frappier remarque que le *cristal* du heaume (vers 141) est de la « verroterie », opinion à laquelle nous souscrivons bien volontiers. Contrairement à G. Raynaud de Lage, *op. cit.*, p. 149, nous traduisons le verbe *relever* du vers 144 par *soutenir* et non par *ramasser* qui nous semble excessif !

158. On ne sait si *Pierrelate* est le village de la Drôme (siège actuel d'une importante usine atomique) ou Peralada, sur le versant espagnol des Pyrénées-Orientales.

163-179. Guillaume évoque ici la scène qui donne son titre au *Couronnement*, mais qui en fait n'est que le début de la chanson puisque le reste rapporte les prouesses de Guillaume, défenseur de Louis ; la lutte commence dès la cérémonie du couronnement, et l'exécution d'Arnéïs est le premier service que Guillaume rend au nouveau roi.

169. Au vers 169, la chapelle Marie-Madeleine désigne bien la chapelle du palais d'Aix où Louis le Débonnaire fut effectivement couronné en 813, mais il était âgé de trente-cinq ans et non de quinze comme le dit l'épopée.

182-200. La trahison d'Acelin et de son père Richard de Normandie est relatée dans le *Couronnement* aux vers 1450-2220

190. En ce qui concerne le vers 190, nous traduisons le texte B qui est aussi celui de D (Paris) : *Si le tuai* et nous abandonnons la version de Perrier : *Si le loai*. On ne sait de quelle grande tour il s'agit au vers 200 ; voir toutefois Raynaud de Lage, *op. cit.*, p. 175.

203-250. Tout ce passage rappelle des faits qui sont longuement exposés dans le *Couronnement*, du vers 2225 au vers 2641. Toutefois, la lutte contre Gui l'Allemand qui occupe une grande place dans le *Couronnement*, se règle ici en quelques vers, tandis que celle où l'adversaire de Guillaume est Oton occupe toute la laisse VIII ; mais cet Oton est une création du *Charroi* : son nom ne figure pas dans le *Couronnement* où l'on mentionne un anonyme « per de Rome ». Jean Frappier, *op. cit.*, traite cette question très complètement et se range à l'avis de Langlois, édition du *Charroi*, S.A.T.F., Paris, 1888, qui estime qu'Oton n'est qu'un nom amené par l'assonance. On consultera les pages 109-111 et surtout 210-212 de l'ouvrage de J. Frappier ; d'autre part la note 2 de la p. 212 apporte tous les éclaircissements nécessaires sur les vers 210-212 du *Charroi* qui sont un peu mystérieux, c'est le moins que l'on en puisse dire ! Quel est cet hôte nommé Gui, lui aussi, qui fait fuir Guillaume par la mer ?

212. Nous avons traduit par *navire*, au vers 212, le mot *dromon* qui est un emprunt au vocabulaire maritime de Byzance. Cf. Raynaud de Lage, *op. cit.*, p. 180.

217. Il est question plusieurs fois dans le *Charroi* du *pré Noiron* ; nous traduisons par *Parc de Néron*. Il s'agit de l'ancien *Ager Vaticanus*, aujourd'hui Prati di Castello ; la tradition veut qu'à cet endroit ou dans son voisinage, saint Pierre ait été crucifié. Ce serait aussi l'emplacement des jardins où Néron, après l'incendie de Rome, fit brûler les chrétiens, les ayant disposés comme des torches.

243. Au vers 243, nous remplaçons *marbre* du texte de Perrier par *mur* qui est dans les manuscrits BCD. Le manuscrit A4 (Milan) remplace *bessié*, baissé, par *mucié*, caché, qui est plus expressif. Dans les *Manants du Roi* (La Favillana), La Varende emploie ce verbe sous la forme *musser* pour donner à son récit une couleur normande et archaïque à la fois.

255. Avec J. Frappier, nous adoptons la leçon de C (v. 309) : *Dant muse en cort m'apelent li Pohier* ; cf. Frappier, *op. cit.*, II, p. 214, note 2. En effet le texte de l'éd. Perrier : *Dont nus en cort m'apelast chevalier* ne paraît pas offrir de sens satisfaisant.

259. Au lieu de *Ne en ta cort* (éd. Perrier), nous traduisons *Dont en ta cort*, avec Cl. Régnier.

260. Cette manière pittoresque de parler signifie que Guillaume n'a pas de porte, partant pas de maison !

266-267. Là encore Guillaume use d'un style très imagé : la lance ennemie qui se plante dans le bouclier devient le clou, le morceau de fer qu'il n'a même pas pu obtenir du roi.

275. Le texte d'ancien français dit littéralement que les péchés de Guillaume lui sont restés dans le « ventre » ; cela signifie : dans le « cœur », au plus profond de lui-même. Nous ne mettons plus, comme au Moyen Age, le cœur dans le ventre, mais nous avons gardé une trace de cette idée dans la locution familière : « avoir du cœur au ventre ». Cf. à ce sujet *The Continuations of the Old French Perceval of Chretien de Troyes*. Vol. III, Part 2, *Glossary of the first continuation* by Lucien Foulet, Philadelphia 1955, The American Philosophical Society, à l'article *vantre*.

320. On perdrait l'image en traduisant platement par « la meilleure femme du monde ». Il est permis aussi de se

demander si le fait de boire du vin n'implique pas, dans la civilisation médiévale, une idée de noblesse de classe.

334. Le mot *vaillissant*, déjà rencontré aux vers 254 et 258, et que l'on retrouvera au vers 403, est employé dans notre texte concurremment avec *vaillant* qui se retrouve aux vers 277, 428 et 1478. Nous avons calqué nos traductions sur l'expression figée qui nous reste de l'ancienne langue : « N'avoir pas un sou vaillant », plus pittoresque que : « N'avoir pas la valeur d'un sou ». Tobler, *Vermischte Beiträge zur französischen Grammatik*, V, 5, fait de *vaillant* un participe présent et de *sou* un complément de prix. Nous regardons aussi *vaillissant* comme un participe présent de forme aberrante.

341. On lit à l'*Index des noms propres* de l'éd. Perrier : « val de Riviers, province des Pays-Bas ».

342. Il s'agit de l'acquittement par composition, en vigueur dans l'ancien droit germanique, c'est-à-dire la compensation en argent d'un meurtre.

388. Nous n'avons pu rendre l'expression *garçon à pié* que par *valet ;* mais s'agit-il de valets d'armée qui sont en quelque sorte des fantassins ou de valets de maison qui appartiennent à la plus basse classe de la domesticité ?

436. Perrier écrit : *Ge l'i ai mis ;* nous corrigeons en : *Ge li ai mis.* On lit dans le *Couronnement :* (*Li cuens la prent... Vient a l'enfant*), *si li assiet el chief* (vers 144). Dans la seconde partie du vers, nous traduisons le futur *vorrai* par un présent en accord avec nos grammairiens contemporains dont Georges Gougenheim.

450-453. Le terme d'Espagne désigne toutes les possessions des Sarrasins ; c'est pourquoi Nîmes et Orange font partie du domaine espagnol. Tortolouse est probablement

Tortosa, sur l'Ebre, en Catalogne ; quant à Portpaillart, il semble difficile à localiser (Cf. J. Frappier, *op. cit.*, II, p. 220, note 3 et M.-J. Barnett, *Porpaillart in the Cycle de Guillaume d'Orange*, in *Modern Lang. Rev.*, LI, 1956, p. 507-511).

454. Nous traduisons le texte de C : *S'il le vos done* au lieu du texte de Perrier : *S'il la vos donne* ; le sens est plus satisfaisant. Il en va de même au vers 485.

505. On peut adopter la leçon de tous les autres manuscrits : *par les desrubes*, alors que le texte de Perrier porte : *por les desrubes* ; on devra traduire dans ce cas : « Là où le Rhône court sur des rochers abrupts ».

510. Au lieu de *la feutreüre*, il faut couper *l'afeutreüre* dans la version de Perrier ; le mot précise *hauberc* comme une sorte d'accusatif de relation.

516-521. Cette énumération surprenante de rois païens dont les noms peuvent venir de la Bible : *Golias*, ou n'être que des sobriquets narquois : *Quinzepaumes*, ou même être français : *Tiebaut*, fait songer à l'onomastique païenne de la *Chanson de Roland*, dont J. Bédier a relevé l'étrangeté dans *La Chanson de Roland commentée*. p. 99.

547. Après ce vers, nous traduisons un vers de transition ajouté par le manuscrit C : *Ne savés pas por coi vos voel laissier ?*

549. Nous adoptons la leçon de C : *Fui a Saint Gille, reving par Monpellier*, car le vers de Perrier : *Fui a Saint Gile, lors fui ge chiés un ber* est suspect par son assonance en *é* dans une laisse en *ié* ; mais surtout, la scène se déroule à Montpellier et le vers 577 le prouve : *Et à saint Gile, dont venoie proier*. Pour que le sens soit entièrement satisfaisant.

nous adoptons également C pour le vers 550 : *un cortois chevalier* au lieu de *le cortois chevalier*.

555. Après ce vers, nous traduisons un vers de transition ajouté par C : *Tot mon chemin voloie repairier*, mais nous abandonnons l'autre vers de transition : *Quant mangié oi moi et mi chevalier* qui serait mal venu après le vers 553 de la version Perrier : *Quant ce fu chose que eüsmes mengié*.

558-559. En accord avec J. Frappier, *op. cit.*, II, p. 224. note 4, nous renonçons au texte Perrier qui fait descendre Guillaume dans un *celier* avant de le faire monter dans un *solier !* La leçon de C est évidemment préférable (v. 628-29) : *Puis me mena en un moult haut solier Et puis après en un plus haut planchier*.

564. Sur cette pseudo-tentative de séduction, cf. notre Bibliographie, étude de M. Mancini, p. 207-208.

630. « Il y a là une inconséquence, écrit J. Frappier, puisque Bertrand n'a jamais refusé d'accompagner Guillaume dans sa guerre contre les Sarrasins et que seul Guielin a été battu par son père. » Le manuscrit C présente les faits plus correctement, mais en allongeant beaucoup la rédaction ainsi que D qui, en outre, offre des variantes particulières ; pour le détail, cf. J. Frappier, *op. cit.*, II, p. 226, note 2.

640. Nous avons gardé dans notre traduction le mot *journal* qui est une mesure de surface ; l'expression technique rurale est *journal de terre*. Cette mesure qui désigne ce que l'on peut labourer en une journée, varie d'une province à une autre. La Varende emploie ce terme expressif dans les *Manants du Roi* (Les derniers chouans) : « mille journaux de terre et pas âme qui vive, dessus... ».

642. La leçon de A1 (Paris) que reproduit Perrier : *As menus cops* est certainement altérée ; il vaut mieux lire :

As roncins clops, en tirant parti des variantes (cf. Perrier, p. 58), et traduire, comme nous l'avons fait, par « aux roussins éclopés ».

648. Ce vers, comme le vers 653, est un refrain, mais il n'interrompt pas le récit : il y est lié au contraire, et c'est pourquoi nous ne l'avons pas isolé.

657. Ici commence une nouvelle laisse. Le même cas se présentera au vers 1047, si bien que notre traduction couvre cinquante-neuf laisses, alors que l'éd. Perrier n'en distingue que cinquante-sept, mais le compte des vers reste le même ; en effet, on l'aura déjà constaté, les vers ajoutés sont mis entre parenthèses et non numérotés, afin de faciliter la lecture conjointe du texte et de la traduction.

727. *Esligïer* est un barbarisme ; il faut suivre la leçon de A4 : *je puisse esligier*, ce que nous faisons.

785. Le voyage de Paris à Nîmes commence. Pour en bien suivre et comprendre les étapes, il est précieux de se servir du tableau de J. Frappier, *op. cit.*, II, p. 234-37.

789. D'après les manuscrits BCD, nous traduisons *Cil queus* et non *Cil qui* de la version Perrier.

792. Notre traduction ne peut rendre compte de l'expression médiévale contenue dans ce vers : *Del cuer del ventre ;* voir cependant notre note du vers 275.

837-838. Nous relevons dans ces deux vers trois substantifs qui désignent le même objet, une tente ; il est bien difficile de traduire d'une manière différente : *tres, paveillons, aucubes.* D'après L. Foulet, *op. cit.*, article *paveillon*, le pavillon devait être une tente plus vaste et plus somptueuse que le *tref* ou *tres*. Quant à *aucube*, nous avons dû renoncer à le traduire : en effet, nos recherches nous ont amené à découvrir

un terme arabe *al gobbah* qui est à l'origine de notre *alcôve*
et aussi d'*aucube* ; donc l'alcôve étant une petite chambre
dans une plus grande chambre à coucher, il est possible
que l'*aucube* soit une très petite tente de couchage, peut-être
même, qui sait, un sac de couchage !

840. Les pélerins pouvaient se rendre à Saint-Gilles
par la voie Regordane ; en ce cas, ils passaient à Brioude
(cf. vers 824) où on leur faisait visiter la basilique de saint
Julien. Les chanoines y avaient déposé des trophées épiques.
Voir les premiers vers de *La Prise d'Orange*, éd. Cl. Régnier,
Paris, Klincksieck, 1967. D'après J. Frappier, *op. cit.*, II,
p. 235, note 3, *Ricordane* (que nous retrouvons aux vers 952
et 957 du *Charroi*) semble désigner non seulement la voie,
mais aussi une région montagneuse au sud de Clermont-
Ferrand. Voir aussi la note 1, p. 190 de l'ouvrage de J. Frappier.

844. Le texte du *Charroi* mentionne ici, parmi les offran-
des de Guillaume, *quatre pailes et trois tapis roez ;* le mot
paile désigne un tissu de soie et l'adjectif *roez* précise que
les tapis sont ornés de dessins en forme de roues, selon L. Foulet, *op. cit.* ; toutes ces étoffes sont d'origine orientale et
nous reviendrons plus loin sur cette question. Cf. cependant
L. Foulet, à l'article *pale 2*.

870. Guielin est dit *senez !* Il s'agit vraiment d'une
épithète « de nature » qui conviendrait mieux à Bertrand,
car tout ce que nous savons du jeune Guielin, à travers les
chansons du cycle de Guillaume, nous le ferait plutôt qualifier
de farceur !

885. L'interprétation du mot *billete* dans le texte est
douteuse. Il s'agit peut-être d'un jeu de bâtonnets.

895-899. Perrier a mal ponctué cette tirade ; pour lui
rendre son sens correct, nous avons placé un point d'excla-

mation à la fin du vers 895 et une virgule à la fin du vers 898.

919. Étymologiquement le vavasseur est vassal d'un vassal et tient sa terre d'un seigneur qui dépend lui-même d'un suzerain.

940. Nous avons traduit *ancrenez* par *percés de trous d'air*, selon le dictionnaire de Tobler-Lommatzsch ; en effet, on retrouve dans ce verbe le thème *cren* d'où vient le bas latin *crena*, entaille, l'ancien français *crenel*, *creneure*, ce dernier terme signifiant fente, ouverture. Les tonneaux doivent avoir de petites ouvertures pour que les chevaliers puissent respirer.

943. Nous traduisons par *grand'route* l'expression *chemin ferré* ; cf. Foulet, *op. cit.*, p. 113.

960. Nous avons traduit l'ancien français : *les charrues doublent*, en nous référant à l'article de Cl. Régnier, « Le mellor de mes bues, Roget, le mellor de me carue » (*Aucassin et Nicolette*, XXIV, 51-52), dans *Mélanges offerts à Jean Frappier*, II, p. 935-43 ; voir en particulier la page 939 pour les vers 960 et 967.

977. Le texte de Perrier a imprimé par erreur *entrepaignent*, alors qu'il s'agit d'*entrepraignent*, du verbe *entreprendre*, faire face à une situation dangereuse (cf. Foulet, *op. cit.*). Ce verbe est repris plus loin (vers 981), au participe passé.

979. Il faut remplacer *escrins* de la version Perrier par *escris*, leçon du manuscrit C ; les Français font deux marques sur certains tonneaux.

986-987. Ces deux vers, comme les vers 968-969, sont un refrain, mais lié au récit.

1024. Nous avons traduit par équipement le mot *corroie*, de sens douteux. Il en va de même au vers 1330.

1038. Nous avons traduit par *violâtre* l'adjectif *perse* ;
ce dernier est en réalité intraduisible, car on ignore absolument de quelle couleur il s'agit. Foulet, *op. cit.*, dont on
pourra consulter avec profit le très intéressant article *pers*,
précise que pour certains, c'est une nuance de bleu, pour
d'autres, c'est le violet. On sait qu'il est difficile de discuter
des couleurs ! Nous appelons *violet* ce que les Anglo-Saxons
appellent *purple* ; mais nous traduisons *purple* par *pourpre* !
Et *pers* peut encore désigner la couleur de l'argile : livide.
Alors ?

1056. *Lavardi* est sans doute un nom altéré. Cf. J. Frappier, *op. cit.*, II, p. 237, note 9.

1064-1065. Ces deux vers énumèrent divers tissus sur
lesquels nous sommes très mal renseignés, en particulier
les *syglatons* qui semblent être des étoffes de soie ou peut-
être plus précisément des brocarts ; G. Moignet, *La chanson
de Roland*, Paris, Bordas, 1969, écrit à la page 82, vers 846,
que le mot est dérivé de l'arabe *siqillat*, « tissu décoré de
sceaux », emprunté au latin *sigillatum* ; il signale, d'autre
part, à propos de l'*écarlate*, qu'il s'agit d'une riche étoffe,
et non d'une couleur, et que le mot a la même origine. Nous
retrouverons l'*écarlate* et les *syglatons* aux vers 1140-1141.
Ajoutons que ces derniers sont orthographiés de diverses
manières dans l'ancienne langue : *sigladon, ciclaton, sciglaton.*

1066. A propos de *verz heaumes*, Cl. Régnier, *op. cit.*,
p. 133 (vers 945), signale que les heaumes étaient peints.

1085. Le narrateur interrompt son récit pour « annoncer
derechef sa chanson », écrit J. Frappier, *op. cit.*, II, p. 243,
« Ce faux prologue peut correspondre à une nouvelle tranche
de récitation ».

1093. Au lieu de *terre*, nous traduisons *voie* d'après le

manuscrit C ; Nîmes, en effet, est sur le chemin de Saint-Gilles. Après le vers 1094 de la version Perrier : *A une part des estres de la vile*, il manque un vers dont l'omission rend incompréhensible le vers 1095 : *Mes a cele heure n'en i avoit il mie*. En conséquence, nous remplaçons le vers 1094 par la traduction des vers 1205-6 du manuscrit D : *En la cités out une place antive, Lai ou l'on ore lou mostier et la Virge*. Nous obtenons ainsi un texte plus clair.

1099. Perrier écrit : *Et si tenoient ;* il faut lire : *Et s'i tenoient* avant de traduire.

1102. En ancien français le *perron* correspond à ce que l'on nomme un *montoir* en équitation moderne.

1139. Nous avons traduit par foulard de soie, l'ancien français *cendal* (pluriel *cendaus* dans notre texte) ; il semble que cette étoffe ait été employée surtout comme doublure. Quand au *boucran* ou *bougran* (pluriel *bouqueranz* dans le texte du *Charroi*) nous l'avons rendu par étoffe de lin : le *boucran* était un tissu d'origine orientale, comme tous ceux que nous avons déjà vus, fabriqué probablement à Boukhara, d'où son nom.

1143. Le vers 1144 tel qu'il est : *Respont Otrans : « Bien vos est, marcheanz »*, empêche l'intelligence du passage ; nous préférons traduire la leçon de C : *Et dist li rois : « Amis, mostré nos ent. »* qui s'adapte mieux au contexte.

1147. Il faut modifier la ponctuation de ce vers dans le texte de Perrier, car il est entièrement prononcé par Otrant ; nous traduisons donc le vers sous la forme suivante : « *Que est ce donc el premier chief devant ?* Un tiret doit être placé au début du vers 1148, précédant la réponse de Guillaume.

1193. La Romagne est alors la région qui s'étend entre le Grand-Saint-Bernard et Rome.

1200. Il s'agit du *Crac des Chevaliers* en Syrie ; J. Frappier, *op. cit.*, II, p. 186-188, l'établit d'une manière absolument convaincante.

1223. Nous traduisons la leçon de BC : *Pleüst Mahom*, et non la version de Perrier : *Pleüst a Deu* qui n'a pas de sens dans la bouche d'Otrant.

1317. La « vulgate » (éd. Perrier) écrit *Otrans* par erreur : il en est de même au vers 1327, comme le montre la suite du récit (vers 1367-68). Il est clair qu'à partir de notre laisse L, c'est Harpin, le plus agressif (cf. vers 1313), coupable de l'abattage des bœufs, qui prend la parole.

1318. Harpin jure par *Mahomez* bien entendu ! Nous abandonnons ici le texte de Perrier qui porte *Damedeus*.

1364. La leçon suivie par Perrier : *Raol de Macre ne sui mes apelé*, est probablement corrompue, puisque Guillaume a dit aux païens qu'il se nommait *Tiacre ;* nous traduisons, en conséquence, la leçon du manuscrit B : *Non de Tÿacre ne sui mie appelé*.

1413-1414. Il est impossible qu'un seul chevalier amène tous les chevaux, et nous étions tenté de traduire le texte de C qui mentionne mille chevaliers : *A tant es vos M. chevalier poignant*, mais une considération nous a retenu : d'où sortiraient ces mille chevaliers puisque Guillaume est enfermé entre les murs de la ville de Nîmes avec une partie de ses compagnons déguisés en marchands ? Il ne pourra communiquer avec le reste de l'armée qu'après la libération de la ville. Nous avons donc, faute de mieux, traduit le texte de la « vulgate » ; toutefois, en ce qui concerne le vers 1414, nous avons échangé le nom de Guielin contre celui de Guillaume, beaucoup plus vraisemblable ici.

1425. C'est le mot *jazerant* que nous traduisons par :

à l'algérienne ; l'adjectif *jaseran* est formé sur le nom arabe d'Alger, *al-Djaza'ir*. Il ne faut pas confondre ici le sens et l'étymologie ; les hauberts sont faits de mailles de fer torses à la mode arabe.

1448-1451. Nous ne pouvons nous empêcher d'admirer la fière réponse d'Otrant : même s'il a peur d'être tué par Guillaume (cf. vers 1433), il se refuse à renier la religion musulmane, et les Français saisis de pitié, et peut-être d'estime, pour lui, le conjurent de prononcer les paroles qui retarderaient sa fin. Mais Guillaume, en fureur, coupe court à cette intervention.

1456. Les Français promettent à Otrant six jours de sursis ; nous nous sommes demandé, sans pouvoir y apporter de réponse, à quoi correspondait ce nombre déterminé de six jours.

1459. La chanson ne donne pas de détails sur l'endroit où se trouvent les personnages ; il semble bien que ce soit à l'intérieur du palais d'Otrant. A. Jeanroy, *op. cit.*, commente ainsi le texte dans son adaptation du *Charroi*, au moment de la fuite d'Otrant (vers 1430 et 1433) : « ... il s'enfuit vers les combles de son palais et allait s'échapper par les toits... ».

BIBLIOGRAPHIE

Il ne s'agit pas ici d'une bibliographie exhaustive, mais seulement d'une liste destinée à faire le point des ouvrages parus récemment sur le *Charroi de Nîmes*, en particulier de ceux qui ont vu le jour après l'étude, unique en la matière, de Jean Frappier, où sont signalés les éditions et les travaux critiques antérieurs à 1967. Nous citons cependant quelques ouvrages anciens, dans la mesure où nous les avons utilisés pour notre travail, telle l'édition de J.-L. Perrier qui va bientôt être remplacée par celle de Duncan McMillan (*sous presse*, éd. Klincksieck).

ÉDITIONS ET TRADUCTIONS

Le Charroi de Nîmes, chanson de geste du XIIe siècle éditée par J.-L. Perrier, Paris, Champion, C.F.M.A., 1931 (imprimé de nouveau en 1968).

Le Charroi de Nîmes, chanson de geste éditée par G. De Poerck, R. Van Deyck et R. Zwaenepoel, Textes et Traitement Automatique sous la direction de G. De Poerck, 2 vol., Saint-Aquilin-de-Pacy, Mallier, 1970.

Manuel pratique d'ancien français par G. Raynaud de Lage, Paris, Picard, 1968 (3e tirage). Il s'agit d'une édition partielle des 421 premiers vers du *Charroi de Nîmes*, avec traduction, d'après l'édition fragmentaire de Paul Meyer dans *Recueil d'anciens textes bas-latins, provençaux et français*, t. II, Paris, 1874-1877.

Il carriaggio di Nîmes, Canzone di gesta del XII secolo, a cura di Giuseppe E. Sansone, Bari, Dedalo Libri, 1969 (édition accompagnée d'une traduction en italien).

Des morceaux choisis ont été donnés notamment par Robert Bossuat (*Extraits des chansons de geste*, Larousse) et par André-Marie Gossart (*Contes et Récits extraits des prosateurs et poètes du Moyen Age*, Nathan).

Une adaptation due à la plume d'Alfred Jeanroy a pour titre : *La geste de Guillaume Fierebrace et de Raynouart au tinel,* dans *Poèmes et récits de la Vieille France,* t. VI, Paris, de Boccard, 1924.

Jean Frappier, *Les Chansons de geste du cycle de Guillaume d'Orange,* t. II, p. 179-253, Paris, S.E.D.E.S., 1967 (seconde édition revue et augmentée).

Madeleine Tyssens, *La geste de Guillaume d'Orange dans les manuscrits cycliques,* Bibliothèque de la Faculté de Philosophie et Lettres de l'Université de Liège, fasc. CLXXVIII, Paris, Les Belles Lettres, 1967, p. 101-123.

Cl. Régnier, *A propos de l'édition du « Charroi de Nîmes »,* dans l'*Information littéraire,* 20e année, janvier-février 1968, no 1, p. 32-33.

A. Adler, *A propos du « Charroi de Nîmes »,* dans *Mélanges offerts à Jean Frappier,* Genève, Droz, 1970, t. 1, p. 9-15.

M. Mancini, *L'édifiant, le comique et l'idéologie dans le Charroi de Nîmes,* dans *Société Rencesvals, IVe Congrès International, Studia Romanica,* 14, Heidelberg, Carl Winter 1969, p. 203-212.

D. McMillan, Compte rendu de G.E. Sansone, *op. cit.,* Bari, Dedalo Libri, 1969, dans *Romania,* t. 91, I, Paris, 1970, p. 114-115.

D. McMillan, Discussion, réponse à G.E. Sansone, *Precisazioni sul Carriaggio di Nîmes,* dans *Romania,* t. 91, 3, Paris, 1970, p. 422-423.

J.-Ch. Payen, *Le « Charroi de Nîmes », comédie épique ?* dans *Mélanges offerts à Jean Frappier,* Genève, Droz, 1970, t. II, p. 891-902.

J.-Ch. Payen, *De la tradition à l'écriture : à propos d'un livre récent,* dans *Le Moyen Age,* no 3-4, 1969, p. 529-539.

Pour une bibliographie plus complète comportant les titres d'ouvrages que nous ne mentionnons pas ici, on se reportera à la *Bibliographie* de G. De Poerck, *op. cit.,* t. I, p. 16-19.

TABLE

Joseph FLOCH, Maître-Imprimeur à Mayenne 19 - 9 - 1980 n° 7197

MISSION ENGLAND
WHAT REALLY HAPPENED?

MISSION ENGLAND — WHAT REALLY HAPPENED?

A Report on the Main Meetings of 1984

by Philip Back

A ministry of World Vision

MARC
EUROPE

British Library Cataloguing in Publication Data

Back, Philip
    Mission England — what really happened? a report.
    1. Evangelistic work — England
    I. Title
    269'.2'0942   BV3777.G7

    ISBN 0–947697–24–1

MARC Europe is an integral part of World Vision, an international Christian humanitarian organisation. MARC's object is to assist Christian leaders with factual information, surveys, management skills, strategic planning and other tools for evangelism. MARC also publishes and distributes related books on mission, church growth, management, spiritual maturity and other topics.

Contents

Foreword

When a group of people ask for (and get) some £2 million from the Churches for an evangelistic enterprise, there needs to be some way of expressing accountability.

We in Mission England felt convinced that an objective study of our work and a published report was the best way to do this. I am very grateful to MARC Europe for being prepared to put their expertise at our disposal.

This is the first report — there is more to come. In a sense what we have here is the easiest to analyse. The main Mission England meetings were conducted by Dr Billy Graham and his team in their well proven 'Crusade' format. They have always been fastidious in keeping and studying the statistics of their work and The Billy Graham Evangelistic Association was more than ready to make its information available to MARC.

The 41 Billy Graham meetings in 1984 were undoubtedly the high spot of Mission England (along with the equally remarkable meetings in Sheffield a year later). They were meant to be. It would be a mistake however to regard them as the sum total of all the evangelism that took place through the 6,000 churches that participated in the Mission England three-year programme.

Without Billy Graham's readiness to face the gruelling 1984 schedule, Mission England could not have happened; and the other activities (such as training, local church evangelism, and especially the promotion of prayer) would not have taken place.

However, I believe that these other aspects of Mission England in turn helped to make Billy Graham's Crusade evangelism even more effective than before. The percentage response to his preaching took us all by surprise — but it was a delightful, and moving surprise!

This report therefore does not cover all the activities of Mission England, but it covers what was certainly the central element (and the most expensive). For that reason a report needs to be prepared; and I am grateful to MARC Europe for doing it so thoroughly.

Gavin Reid,
National Director,
Mission England.
October 1985

Introduction

1984 was a unique year in the history of the Christian church in England. No fewer than seven major evangelistic events were held in different parts of the country, using the services of two of the world's best-known evangelists — Luis Palau and Billy Graham. The degree of interest aroused by this activity was quite remarkable and the response generated by the preaching of the gospel totally unprecedented in the modern age.

This report has been prepared at the request of, and specifically for, the Mission England Federal Board, who believe the findings warrant a wider audience. It is important to recognise at the outset that it is limited in its scope and does not therefore represent a full picture of the summer of 1984, nor indeed of the Mission England programme of which the events I describe formed only a part. In the first place, of course, this book deals only with Mission England; Luis Palau's completely independent campaign in the capital is not discussed here and will be the subject of a separate publication. Secondly, this report only covers the six major missions led by Billy Graham during the summer of 1984 and held in Bristol, Sunderland, Norwich, Birmingham, Liverpool and Ipswich. Sheffield, then, is not included; neither are the many missions by video and other outreach events held across the country under the auspices of Mission England.

This report is, essentially, a statistical document. The powerful testimonies of transformed lives are told elsewhere, and will no doubt lead others to the same responses, but this book does not deal in individuals so much as in the patterns which emerge from their being grouped together in different ways. We do not seek to convey an impression that a person responds other than as an individual to a personal challenge from the Holy Spirit; but we believe that there are important characteristics of this type of outreach that ought to be set out.

The analysis which follows examines patterns in the attendance and response at the six cited Mission England events by reference to selected factors which might have been influential. It also examines the types of response which individuals were led to make, and the characteristics of those who went forward. Finally, the report explores factors such as the predisposition of people to travel to events like this, and the geographical distribution of those who responded, identifying areas particularly touched by the Mission.

Much of the information which has been used to compile the report was drawn from the individual counsellor forms which were completed when a person went forward at Dr Graham's invitation. The data which has been extracted from these forms for this purpose was:

> age
> sex
> type of response being made
> denominational background
> occupation
> postcode

It will be noted that none of this information is sufficient to allow identification of any individual respondent and in no instance were confidential data disclosed that would have made such identification possible. Additional information has been taken from Mission England records and other publications, and due credit is given in the text.

Mention should be made of the treatment of errors and missing information. Generally, forms which were known to contain errors, or where incomplete information was given, have been ignored. Where the volume of these is substantial, and has the potential to influence the stated result, appropriate comment has been made in the text. In particular, it was noted that a substantial number of forms from the Bristol Mission went astray, and the figures were consequently not available to us.

Obviously there are other significant omissions. The vast range of other events linked to Mission England are beyond the scope of the report, as are the many personal responses made in the privacy of people's own homes and therefore not recorded by counsellors. Dramatic as the statistics presented here are, it must be remembered that they represent considerably less than the total impact of the campaign.

What, then, are the essential aims of a report like this? There are two basic answers:

> the report explains, in part, a remarkable series of meetings, aiming at an understanding of precisely what took place in numerical terms;

> the report also identifies some of the characteristics of the English people in the context of large evangelistic campaigns, showing both the effectiveness and the limitations of such events. It may therefore be seen as an invaluable aid to planning future events of this type.

Prayers for national revival have been offered regularly in many churches in England for a considerable period of time. The report suggests that there is a sense in which Mission England is an answer to those prayers; but it is by no means the whole answer. The statistics here should cause all English Christians to glorify God for what He has done in our midst, but they should also make us stop and think. How adequate are our churches to cope with the continuing spiritual needs of the numbers who responded in 1984? And what about the others? Even after Mission England, the overwhelming majority of people in England do not attend church, and have little exposure to the gospel message. Perhaps, then, there is a third aim in a report like this: to draw our attention to the vast mission field that lies on our very doorsteps.

I am grateful to the Mission England board for allowing this report to be published, and to my colleagues at MARC whose invaluable comments and suggestions appear throughout. Errors of fact or interpretation are, of course, my responsibility.

Philip Back
MARC Europe
October 1985

ATTENDANCE
AND GENERAL RESPONSE

Attendance — National

During the summer of 1984, over a million people passed through the turnstiles to attend one or other of the 41 Mission England meetings – the equivalent of around 2%, or 1 in 50, of the entire population of England and Wales. Whilst this comparison helps to convey the overall dimension of the campaign, it must be remembered that the figure will include a significant number of individuals who attended more than one meeting; it is also evident from the counsellor forms that some Scots and Irish residents were present. On the other hand, and most significantly, it should be pointed out that no Mission England meetings were held in London and the South East, the most densely populated region of the UK.

The attendance at the major mission events is, of course, only part of the picture, as this figure does not include the estimated audience of 311,000 at the video and associate evangelist ministry meetings which were held between May and July 1984 under the auspices of Mission England. The total number of people who heard the gospel preached as a result of Mission England is thus in excess of 1,300,000, corresponding to nearly 3% of the population of England and Wales, and demonstrating a remarkable degree of interest in the Christian message.

The level of attendance at each of the Mission England meetings varied considerably, but never fell below 10,000; indeed only 4 of the 41 meetings reported attendances less than 15,000. The three best attended meetings were at Birmingham on 6th July, when 39,000 were present, at Bristol on 19th May when 38,112 attended, and at Liverpool on 17th July where the attendance was 37,892. The average attendance over all 41 meetings was 25,039.

Attendance — Local

Table 1: Total and average daily attendance at each location

Location	Total attendance	No of meetings	Average daily attendance
Birmingham	257,015	8	32,127
Liverpool	247,989	8	30,999
Bristol	244,008	8	30,501
Ipswich	90,363	5	18,073
Norwich	63,128	4	15,782
Sunderland	124,097	8	15,512
National	1,026,600	41	25,039

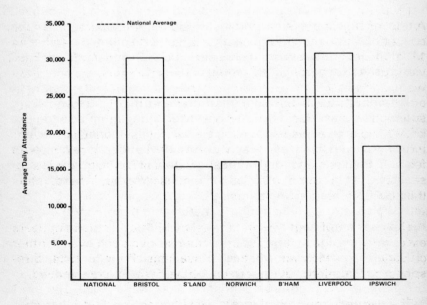

Although the national figures give a good overall impression of the impact of Mission England, examination of the attendance at each of the six locations reveals some interesting features. The best attended of the six missions were those held in Birmingham, Bristol and Liverpool, where the total attendance over each of the eight-day missions was approximately a quarter of a million, and where the daily attendance was consistently in excess of 30,000. The directors of Bristol City FC in particular must have looked enviously at the drawing power of Dr Graham, considering the average home attendance of less than 5,000 for the usual entertainment at Ashton Gate.

What is also apparent from this data is the very wide gap between these three missions and those in Ipswich, Norwich and Sunderland. The two East Anglian missions were considerably shorter than the others, and this — together with the size of the immediate population — goes some way to explaining the lower total attendances. The other eight-day mission, at Sunderland, attracted the fourth largest total attendance, but the figure is only around half the attendance at the other eight-day missions and Sunderland in fact produced the lowest average daily attendance. Possible reasons for this will be examined further elsewhere in this report.

Overall Response — National

A total of 96,982 people went forward for further counselling in the course of Mission England, representing 9.4% (approximately 1 in 11) of those who attended the meetings. The counsellor forms provided us with a thorough breakdown of precisely who the enquirers were, and this will be explored in some detail later in the report. In addition to these, it was estimated that a further 8,000 people responded at the video missions, and to this one must add the unknown number of respondents at the associate evangelists' meetings. It is also reasonable to suppose that a number of people who felt unable to come forward at the invitation of Dr Graham will subsequently have sought independent counselling, or, indeed, made their own private commitment to Christ.

The number of enquiries generated by Mission England appears exceptionally high in terms of the response levels achieved in other crusades for which information is available. Prior to 1984, a response of 5% might have been thought very satisfactory indeed.

The numbers counselled each day at Mission England varied considerably, from 667 at Norwich on 12th June, to 5,034 at Birmingham on 6th July — a figure which must have caused some headaches for those organising the counsellor teams. On average, 2,365 people were counselled for each meeting held.

Table 2: Enquirers counselled at each location

Location	Total no of enquirers	No of meetings	Average daily enquirers
Liverpool	27,412	8	3,427
Birmingham	26,181	8	3,273
Bristol	20,444	8	2,556
Ipswich	7,458	5	1,492
Sunderland	11,785	8	1,473
Norwich	3,702	4	926
National	96,982	41	2,365

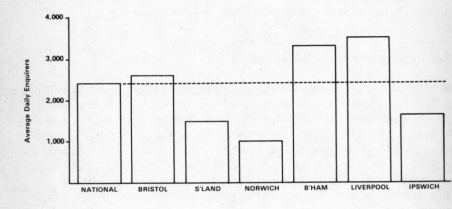

Response – Local

The greatest number of enquirers came forward in the course of the Liverpool campaign, where a total of 27,412 responded to Dr Graham's invitation and where, on average, 3,427 people were counselled each day. As would be expected, the other two best attended missions, at Birmingham and Bristol, also produced higher enquiry numbers and daily averages. It is, nevertheless, interesting that Liverpool, which was second by a significant margin to Birmingham in terms of attendance, should lead the table insofar as the number of enquirers is concerned. Similarly, Sunderland, which was the least well attended mission on average, is far from bottom in terms of average daily enquirers.

Table 3 shows what may be termed the 'enquiry rate', which represents simply the percentage of those attending who subsequently went forward for further counselling. The figures are quite remarkable: 1 in 9 of those present at the Liverpool mission went forward, and the response at the other missions is also exceptional in terms of the experience from previous campaigns of this type. Even the relatively low enquiry rate at Norwich should be put into perspective by setting it against what might have been expected given enquiry rates achieved at earlier crusades.

Table 3: 'Enquiry rate': enquirers as a percentage of attendance

Location	Enquiry rate
Liverpool	11.1%
Birmingham	10.2%
Sunderland	9.5%
Bristol	8.4%
Ipswich	8.3%
Norwich	5.9%
National	9.4%

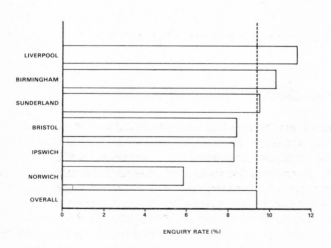

An interesting feature which emerges from this study is the 9.5%

enquiry rate at Sunderland, which as Table 1 shows, was the least well attended of the six missions. Whilst the attendance may have been disappointing to the organisers in terms of what was achieved elsewhere, great encouragement should be taken from the responsiveness of those who did attend. Conversely, although Bristol was one of the best attended missions, the enquiry rate was only two-thirds that which was reported at the other large missions. It would be appropriate to explore possible reasons for such a wide variation in enquiry rate.

The highest enquiry rate for any individual meeting was recorded at Sunderland on 28th May when 14.5% of the people in the stadium — about 1 in 7 — braved the coldest late spring bank holiday since records began to respond to Dr Graham's invitation. Derek Williams has pointed out that this is the highest level of response ever recorded for a Billy Graham meeting in England, possibly exceeding anything the team has experienced elsewhere in the world. Some 60% of those who went forward expressed a desire to know Jesus as Saviour (against a national average of 55.6%) and those who were disappointed at the lowest attendance of the entire summer should take heart at the evidence that those who did attend had a genuine hunger for the gospel that Billy Graham proclaimed.

Other exceptional enquiry rates were recorded at Birmingham on 6th July (12.9%) and at Sunderland again on 1st June (12.7%); in all, thirteen of the forty-one meetings (including all eight at Liverpool) reported enquiry rates in excess of 10%. The lowest levels of response were all at Norwich on 10th June (4.7%), 12th June (5.1%) and 11th June (6.2%).

Attendance and Response by Day of the Week

It is worth examining the attendance figures in more detail to determine whether there is any consistent pattern of attendance levels on particular days of the week. Similarly, there is merit in looking further at the enquiry rate to see whether there is any consistent fluctuation according to the particular day on which a meeting is held.

Four of the six separate missions held in connection with Mission England ran for a period of eight consecutive days in each case, beginning and ending on Saturdays. Attendance levels and enquiry rates varied quite markedly between the opening Saturday of an

18

eight day mission and the closing Saturday, and these two days have therefore been identified separately for purposes of this analysis. The mission at Norwich ran for four days, commencing on an (opening) Saturday and finishing on a Tuesday, whilst the mission at Ipswich began on a Tuesday and ran for five days, to end on a (closing) Saturday.

Meetings were held on Sundays at five of the six venues, the exception being the Ipswich mission. All weekday meetings were, for obvious reasons, held in the evening, but some weekend meetings were held in the afternoon. Unfortunately the number of such meetings is too small to allow us to examine conclusively the effect of the timing of a meeting on attendance independently of the other significant contributory factors. The period of the mission coincided with only one Bank Holiday, on 28th May, when, interestingly, the lowest attendance of any individual meeting was recorded at Sunderland. Whether this was due more to the fact of the holiday, or to the appallingly cold weather, is a matter for speculation.

Whilst the national averages give an overall impression, the wide disparity in attendance level between the three largest missions and the others may mean that some exceptionally large congregations are distorting the true picture. It is therefore necessary to examine each of the individual missions individually to detect any patterns of

Table 4: Attendance and enquiry rate by day of the week

Day	Average attendance	Enquiry rate
Opening Saturday	24,638	9.0%
Sunday	20,113	8.4%
Monday	23,678	9.3%
Tuesday	24,065	9.0%
Wednesday	28,274	9.1%
Thursday	23,564	9.2%
Friday	28,854	11.3%
Closing Saturday	27,321	9.8%
All days	25,039	9.4%

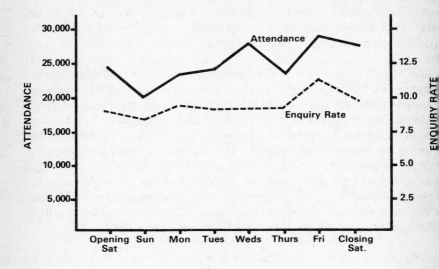

Table 5: Highest and lowest daily attendances at each location

Location (length)	Highest attendances	Days	Lowest attendances	Days
Bristol (8)	38,112	Closing Sat	25,127	Sunday
	36,504	Friday	25,511	Thursday
Sunderland (8)	20,363	Wednesday	10,636	Sunday
	19,032	Closing Sat	10,766	Monday
Norwich (4)	18,194	Sunday	13,133	Tuesday
Birmingham (8)	39,000	Friday	27,915	Thursday
	33,986	Wednesday	29,384	Sunday
Liverpool (8)	37,892	Tuesday	17,224	Sunday
	35,415	Friday	27,051	Opening Sat
Ipswich (5)	20,032	Wednesday	16,452	Tuesday

20

attendance, and Table 5 shows the highest and lowest daily attendances at each of the six locations. The two highest and two lowest attendance figures are quoted for each of the eight-day missions, and the highest and lowest attendance figures are quoted for the two shorter East Anglian missions. In each case, the day of the week on which these high and low attendances were recorded is noted, and it is interesting to see that the local figures, at least for the eight day missions, confirm the overall impression given by the national averages. Friday, Wednesday, and closing Saturday emerge as consistently among the best attended days at each of the eight day missions, and also at Ipswich; paradoxically, Sunday shows up as the best attended day at Norwich, where one must remember there were no Friday, Wednesday or closing Saturday meetings. As regards lowest attendances, there is again a consistency in the appearance of Sunday, Monday and Thursday, although this was not the experience at either of the East Anglian missions, where Tuesday was worst in both cases. Again, one should remember that there were no Sunday or Monday meetings at Ipswich.

At Liverpool in particular, and to a lesser extent at Sunderland, the congregation on the Sunday was remarkably small in comparison with the overall attendance at these venues. In the case of Liverpool, it was later suggested that the explanation for this might lie in the timing of the meeting — in the evening, shortly after the customary end of church services. This, it was felt, might have allowed insufficient time for churchgoers to reach the stadium; the timing might even have inhibited invitation to those unsaved friends who would not have wanted to go to church as well.

Although it is evident from these figures that Sunday is by far the worst attended day of the week, the average Sunday attendance of 20,113 is by no means derisory; it should not be inferred from this analysis that the Sunday rally is in any way superfluous or ineffective.

To a certain extent, these findings conflict with observations made elsewhere, which suggest another factor at work even more influential than the day of the week itself. The conclusion is nevertheless that the day of the week does influence the size of the congregation, and due regard should be paid to this, not least in connection with the attendance of counsellors.

The fact that the highest and lowest enquiry rates are reported for those days which show the highest and lowest average attendances suggests a degree of correlation between congregational size and responsiveness which is difficult to explain. Closer examination of the figures, however, belies this inference; in fact the highest individual enquiry rate of all — 14.5% — was reported at the Bank Holiday meeting already mentioned — which showed the lowest attendance of the entire summer.

In the absence of any third factor having a particular influence on the responsiveness of the congregation, one would imagine that although congregational size might rise and fall by day of the week, responsiveness as measured by enquiry rate would remain fairly constant; that is to say, the percentage of the total attendance who went forward would not fluctuate widely. As the graph shows, however, this is far from being the case. Although the enquiry rate remains steady, around the 9.1% mark for much of the week, there is an evident trough on Sunday, coinciding with a reduced attendance on that day, and similarly a peak on Friday and closing Saturday which appears to correspond with the higher attendance figures noted for those days. One possible explanation for this finding is a possible variation, by day of the week, in the proportion of the congregation who were already Christians. Although some surveys were carried out on people entering the stadium, these were not directed specifically at Christian commitment, and no reliable figures are available which would enable us to determine the level of prior commitment in any given congregation. It would be very interesting to examine this question more closely in future campaigns of this type; in the meantime we can only suggest that larger than usual numbers of non-committed individuals were present on Fridays, whilst Sunday audiences contained larger than average numbers of people with definite Christian commitment.

Weather

The vagaries of the British climate are such that they can seriously affect the outdoor pursuits of the population. In the case of an event such as Mission England, the influence of the weather on a particular day is limited; a large proportion of those attending the meetings will have come by prior arrangement with friends or on organised bus excursions planned some time in advance. Weather conditions nevertheless do have the potential to deter the casual visitor to a mission. When it comes to response, however, weather can play a significant part. It takes some considerable resolution of purpose to stand in the pouring rain waiting for counselling, and there is a sense in which it is much easier to make a response of the type Billy Graham encourages on a pleasant summer's evening.

Table 6 shows the effect of weather conditions both on attendance and enquiry rate. Weather observations were made by people present at the time, and are not objective meteorological information; consequently it must be borne in mind that words like 'cool' are relative to the time of the year, which is probably the way that most people judge the temperature in any event.

Table 6: Effect of weather conditions

Approx. temp	No of days	Average attendance	Enquiry rate
Warm	9	30,613	10.0%
Mild	10	29,696	10.3%
Cool	16	22,203	8.4%
Very cold	6	16,479	9.1%

Weather	No of days	Average attendance	Enquiry rate
Dry	33	26,793	9.6%
Showery	6	16,015	8.1%
Heavy rain	2	23,168	9.1%
All days	41	25,039	9.4%

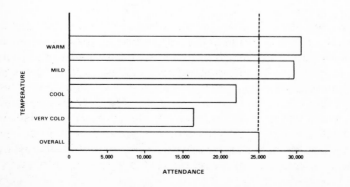

23

From the statistical point of view, there was a reasonably good distribution of different temperatures; this allows us to draw some tentative conclusions. It will be observed from Table 6 that the average attendance on warm and mild days was fairly similar, and considerably higher than the average attendance on cool and very cold days, of which there were a similar number. It is also interesting to note that average attendance falls when the temperature does. These conclusions must, however, be qualified because other factors could be influencing the results. For example, five of the six 'very cold' days were observed at Sunderland; it is open to question whether the low attendances recorded at this particular mission were due more to the temperature or, as one commentator suggests, to a genuine lack of enthusiasm for the mission in the North East of the country.

The picture is less clear with regard to the level of response. The enquiry rate tended to be higher with warmer temperatures and lower with colder ones, but the table shows that an 8.4% enquiry rate on cool days was exceeded on the very cold days, due largely to the responsiveness of the Sunderland audiences, in contrast to their East Anglian counterparts. Generally, it is felt that these results do not allow us to draw any firm conclusions regarding the effect of temperature on responsiveness.

As regards rainfall, the results are inconclusive because there were too few rainy days to allow any pattern to emerge. Whilst this may be unfortunate from the statistical point of view, it is undoubtedly an answer to the prayers of the organisers — for which we should all thank God. Five of the eight days on which rain was reported occurred during the Sunderland mission, and this together with the temperature must have been a major factor in the low average attendance for this eight-day mission.

Enquiry rates were generally lower on rainy days, but again there is insufficient data to draw firm conclusions. The Wednesday night meeting at Bristol, when it was very wet, had a fairly low enquiry rate of 7.3%; on the other hand, a quite remarkable 12.7% enquiry rate was reported at Sunderland on 1st June, in driving rain. Evidently there were many at this meeting for whom the challenge posed overrode considerations of personal comfort.

Ground facilities, and in particular the extent of covered seating accommodation, are not examined in any depth in this report, but are nevertheless worth considering in this context. Even more important than the existence of these facilities is the level of awareness of them amongst those contemplating attendance. Many of those who went to Mission England meetings will doubtless have found themselves in such stadiums for the first time, and may not have been aware that they would be able to enjoy the occasion under shelter. Where such facilities are available — and it is acknowledged that seating in particular was limited at some of the venues — this should be made clear in the advance publicity to overcome any misconceptions in the public mind.

Youth Emphasis Nights

Nine of the forty-one Mission England meetings were designated 'Youth Emphasis Nights', and it was made clear in advance publicity that these would be occasions when the proceedings would be of particular relevance to young people. At the eight-day rallies, the youth emphasis nights were consistently the Tuesday and Friday evening meetings, and there was a youth emphasis night on Wednesday at Ipswich. None of the Norwich events were specifically designated for young people.

How successful were these occasions in their stated purpose of attracting the young? The following table shows that the average attendance on youth emphasis night was considerably higher than at other meetings, particularly so in the case of the Friday events. Whether this is due to the particular emphasis given to these meetings, or to the day of the week, cannot be conclusively judged; Friday is probably a convenient evening for a larger number of people from all age-groups, but the generally good levels of attendance on Tuesdays, as opposed to (say) Mondays or Thursdays, may be due to the specific appeal to young people. Observations taken at similar events tend to reinforce this view.

The enquiry rate on youth nights was also generally higher than on other occasions, particularly on Fridays. Later in this report it will be demonstrated that a very large proportion of the enquirers were young people, and therefore it may reasonably be concluded that the higher enquiry rate on youth emphasis nights is due to the presence of larger than usual numbers of young people.

Table 7: Attendance and enquiry rate by type of meeting

	Attendance	No of events	Average attendance	Enquiry rate
Tuesday youth nights	114,827	4	28,707	9.5%
Friday youth nights	126,237	4	31,559	11.9%
All youth nights	261,096	9	29,011	10.6%
Other meetings	765,504	32	23,922	9.1%
Overall	1,026,600	41	25,039	9.4%

ATTENDANCE   ENQUIRY RATE (%)

Although we are unable directly to compare the age-groups of those responding on youth and other nights, some indication of the position may be gained by examining the occupations of those who went forward. The majority of students are young people, and the proportion of enquirers who gave this as their occupation may be taken as an indicator of the numbers of young people going forward. The figures in question are presented in Table 8.

It will readily be seen that whilst at Mission England as a whole just under half the enquirers gave their occupation as 'students', the proportion who did so on youth nights was well in excess of this. There is therefore a strong suggestion that more young people responded on youth nights than on other occasions, and that the youth emphasis events were successful in bringing the message to the young. It has to be said, nevertheless, that a substantial proportion of the respondents at youth emphasis nights were not young people, and there was clearly also a challenge for those in older age-groups at these events; equally, a substantial proportion of those responding at other meetings were 'students'.

Table 8: Age of enquirers by type of meeting

| | Percentage of enquirers who were: | |
	Students	Non-students
Youth nights	57%	43%
Other meetings	45%	55%
Overall	49%	51%

PERCENTAGE OF ENQUIRERS

Message Theme

Although each of the forty-one messages preached by Dr Graham in the course of Mission England was accompanied by an invitation to personal commitment, different themes were taken as the subject of these messages. In a number of cases, however, the same theme was used more than once, and six themes were used on three or more occasions. It may be of interest to examine the responsiveness of the congregation to each of these themes, which are listed in Table 9.

No theme was used more than once at any of the missions, but it will be noted that John 3:16 was used at each of the local missions, and in fact formed the subject of the opening night address on each occasion. Dr Graham preached from verses in Galatians 5 and 6 at each of the missions other than Bristol, on the subject of the cross of Christ, whilst two other themes were used on four occasions and a further two on three occasions.

27

Table 9: Enquiry rate for selected message themes

Text	Subject	No. of occasions	Enquiry rate (%)
Mark 8: 31–38	The value of a soul	4	10.4%
Mark 10: 17–31	The rich young ruler	4	9.8%
Galatians 5 & 6	The cross	5	9.5%
John 3:16	John 3:16	6	8.9%
Luke 15: 11–32	The prodigal son	3	8.6%
John 3: 1–15	Born into God's family	3	8.3%

Average enquiry rate for all message themes: 9.4%

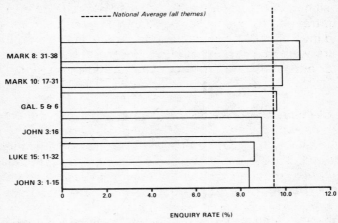

It is noteworthy that the proportion of enquirers who responded to John 3:16 as a message theme is 8.9%, which is somewhat below the national average of 9.4%. It must be remembered, however, that John 3:16 was invariably the opening night topic, and it may well have been the case that the attendance on these occasions included a larger than average number of individuals who had already made a Christian commitment.

The table shows that the subject which drew the highest response was 'The value of a soul', based on the words of Jesus from Mark 8, 'What does it profit a man...'; one wonders whether the evident interest in this theme reflects a growing disillusionment with the materialism that pervades British society.

Some caution must be exercised in interpreting these figures. The fact that lower numbers responded to particular themes should not be taken as suggesting that these topics are less pertinent than their more fruitful counterparts. They were undoubtedly proclaimed under the same spiritual direction and with the same authority, and indeed may well have won individuals for whom other themes might have posed less of a challenge.

Church and individual involvement

The involvement of local churches and individual Christians in an event like Mission England is an absolutely crucial element in the equation. The Billy Graham team's tremendous organisational effort in setting up and running the campaign would have meant little were it not for the activity of Christians up and down the country praying, training as counsellors, organising excursions to the rallies, and inviting their friends to attend. Again, after going forward, enquirers were referred to co-operating churches in their home areas for encouragement in their faith and further spiritual assistance.

Derek Williams records the involvement of 4,750 churches with the Mission, whilst the number of individuals participating in some 'official' capacity was given as 114,000. This number includes those who attended classes in counselling or caring for new Christians, counsellors at the rallies, choir members, stewards and voluntary staff. It undoubtedly includes some people more than once; but it cannot take into account the many thousands who played their part by praying for their unsaved friends, inviting their neighbours, or discussing the issues further on the bus home.

Such information as is available in this area (*Mission to London Phase I: Who Responded?* Peter Brierley, MARC Europe: London, 1984) strongly suggests that those who come to events like Mission England by invitation are much more likely to respond than those who come alone or on impulse. Enquirers at Mission England were not asked what had caused them to come to the meetings; we are therefore unable to assess the extent to which this is true for the Billy Graham campaign. This type of information would nevertheless be of great value in promoting future missions, and it would therefore be worth considering the relatively simple incorporation of a suitably worded question in future counsellor forms.

Other Contributory Factors

Many factors which may have had a bearing on attendance or responsiveness are incapable of measurement, whilst for others insufficient information is available to us to allow assessment of their importance. These factors are nevertheless listed below, for the sake of a more complete picture.

Time of meeting   Most of the Mission England meetings were held in the evenings, commencing at 7.45 for 8 o'clock, but some afternoon meetings were held at weekends. The number of such meetings is, however, too small for us to draw reliable conclusions from attendance figures. It may be worthwhile to review the timing of weekend meetings in the light of the generally lower attendance on Sundays, although it should also be recognised that the timing should make allowance for the large numbers of people who attend after travelling long distances.

Soloists and musicians   A number of different artists participated in the Mission England meetings, but most of these would not be widely known outside the Christian sphere. The exception of course is Cliff Richard, who consistently draws crowds significantly larger than average. We do not have details of the artists participating at individual meetings; research at other events suggests that, apart from Cliff Richard, the presence of any given Christian artist does not materially affect the attendance on a particular occasion.

Ground facilities   We have not considered in any depth the attractiveness, in terms of personal comfort and available facilities, of each of the football grounds selected for Mission England. Public knowledge of the extent of covered seating accommodation at these grounds may well be a factor in attendance levels. It is worth noting under this heading that the directors of Norwich City FC specifically requested Mission England not to allow people to encroach upon the playing surface, as it was feared they would damage it. Those wishing to respond to the messages were therefore asked to convene on the perimeter track, from which stewards prevented access to the pitch itself. Some of those who attended felt that this may have been a factor in the lower response rate at this mission, as the space in the perimeter track was limited, and some people may have been inhibited by the crush and the presence of so many stewards.

Conflicting events   Whilst the organisers were naturally careful to avoid unnecessary conflict with major local events, some clashes were inevitable. No details of these are available, but local organisers may wish to consider this matter independently.

Advance publicity   All of the Mission England campaigns were extensively publicised before and during the local missions, although the final day of the Ipswich mission was only added in June. It goes without saying that the advance publicity will have played a significant part in determining attendance levels, but we are unable to quantify the effectiveness of the different kinds of publicity as no survey was taken of those entering the stadium to find out what had prompted them to come. The additional question already proposed for the counsellor forms would be invaluable to those co-ordinating publicity by establishing the relative effectiveness of the different media — including word of mouth — that were used.

THE RESPONSES MADE

Overall Response

Up to this point, the term 'enquirer' has been used to describe all who went forward for whatever reason in response to Billy Graham's appeal. The counsellor forms included provision for recording the type of response an individual was making, in four broad categories:

Accepting Jesus Christ as personal Saviour. For the sake of brevity, this type of response is described as 'acceptance' in the tables which follow.

To receive assurance of salvation. This has been abbreviated to 'assurance' in the tables.

To rededicate their lives to Christ, suggesting a commitment made at some time in the past. This category has been abbreviated to 'rededication'.

For other reasons, which included providing moral support to a friend, going forward for prayer or other help, requests for further information and literature, and so on. These have been designated 'other'.

It will be evident from a comparison between the figures that follow with the enquirer numbers already cited in this report that there is a disparity. The difference may be accounted for by reference to incomplete counsellor forms, enquirers for whom no form was completed, and to lost or misplaced forms. There is no particular reason why missing elements of information should distort any of the results, and the percentage of forms available allows for reliable conclusions. We have had to assume, however, that the missing batches of forms from Bristol would not materially affect our findings.

The table below shows the types of response made by those enquirers for whom the information is available, representing some 84% of the total of those who went forward.

Table 10: Types of response made by enquirers at all meetings

Type of response	No of enquirers	Percentage of total
Acceptance	45,368	56%
Assurance	11,703	14%
Rededication	14,018	17%
Other	10,748	13%
All responses	81,837	100%

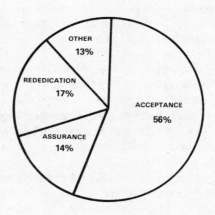

The table indicates that 45,368 people came to a saving faith in Jesus as a result of Mission England. The true figure is almost certainly higher, as a number of those for whom counsellor forms are not available will also have responded in this way. A census of the church taken by MARC Europe in 1979 suggested that the average attendance (adults and children combined) at a church in England was 112; on this basis, the number of those accepting Christ as Saviour is the approximate equivalent of 400 new churches in the country, or 10 new churches for each of the Mission England meetings — quite astounding statistics.

34

The emphasis of Mission England on reaching the unconverted is demonstrated by the percentage figures in the table above, which show that 56% of those who went forward did so to make a first-time commitment.

There was, nevertheless, a definite challenge also to those who had made some form of prior commitment, as seen from the numbers who were seeking assurance of their salvation or who wished to rededicate their lives to the Lord. Those seeking assurance accounted for 14% of the total, whilst 17% of the enquirers at Mission England wished to rededicate themselves. 13% went forward for other reasons.

Table 11 shows the breakdown of these figures between the six area missions, where the column headed 'N' indicates the total number of counsellor forms examined.

It will be seen that, with one or two exceptions, the percentages at each of the local missions are broadly similar to the national picture as a whole.

At Bristol, 54% of those who went forward did so to make a first-time commitment. This is the only one of the eight-day missions to have a figure below the national average in this respect, and it is evident that the figures here are compensated for by a higher percentage of enquirers wishing to rededicate themselves to the Lord. Bristol was the first of the area missions, and may well have drawn a higher number of people who had already made a Christian commitment — possibly at an earlier Billy Graham event. The numbers seeking assurance of salvation or going forward for other reasons were in line with the national average.

At Sunderland, the figures are very similar to the national picture, and confirm that large numbers of previously unreached people responded to Dr Graham's message, despite the reputation of the area as an evangelists' graveyard.

The largest variations from the national norm are seen at Norwich, where the percentage accepting Christ as Saviour is much lower than elsewhere. This is offset by an increased number seeking either assurance of salvation or to rededicate themselves, suggesting that a higher than average proportion of the attendance at the East Anglia North Mission was composed of people with some measure of prior commitment. It is not known how many of these had an active church connection at the time of the mission, but these figures do confirm that Dr Graham's preaching posed a challenge not only to the unconverted but also to the backsliding and uncertain.

Table 11: Comparison of responses at each mission

Location	N(=100%)	Acceptance	Assurance	Rededication	Other
Bristol	14,287	54%	14%	19%	13%
Sunderland	11,477	56%	14%	18%	12%
Norwich	3,287	49%	17%	20%	14%
Birmingham	23,422	57%	15%	15%	13%
Liverpool	22,924	56%	13%	17%	14%
Ipswich	6,440	53%	16%	18%	13%
National	81,837	56%	14%	17%	13%

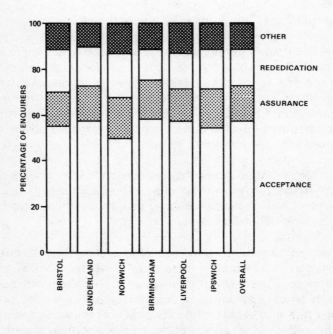

At Birmingham the appeal was much more to the unconverted, with 57% of those going forward seeking to know Christ as Saviour. At this mission, only 15% of the respondents wished to rededicate themselves, a figure which suggests that greater numbers of previously unreached people attended these rallies. At Liverpool, the percentages are again very much along the lines of the national picture.

As with the Norwich meetings, the Ipswich mission shows a comparatively low percentage of enquirers wishing to make any first-time commitment, with a correspondingly higher percentage seeking either assurance of salvation or rededication. Do the figures from East Anglia reflect a higher degree of Christian influence in the past, or were the missions simply a little less successful in drawing those without some form of prior spiritual experience? The results may be related to the size of the towns in which the meetings were held and the shorter duration of the missions in East Anglia. Neither of these places sees many major Christian events of this type, and at Norwich in particular the presence of Dr Graham must have been of considerable interest to Christians who went, perhaps, not so much to hear the Gospel as to participate in the Mission England experience.

Type of Response and Age

Were there any variations in the type of response made according to the age of the enquirer? The counsellor forms asked for an indication of age-group, and counsellors were able to record this information for more than four-fifths of the enquirers. Table 12 breaks the information presented in Table 10 down according to the age-group of the respondents. It is evident that age is a material factor in determining the type of response likely to be made. The difference between adults on the one hand and children and young people on the other shows up even more clearly in the summary presented in Table 13. Almost two-thirds of the respondents in the younger age-group wished to accept Christ as Saviour. This proportion fell to just below half in the case of adult enquirers. The compensating factor is the proportion wishing to rededicate themselves to the Lord; only 10% of those in the younger age-group expressed this reason for going forward, whilst amongst adults nearly a quarter wished to respond in this way. The proportions enquiring about assurance of salvation and for other reasons do not vary to any significant degree between these two age-groups.

37

Table 12: Type of response made by individuals in different age-groups (national)

Age-group	Percentage of enquirers				
	Acceptance	Assurance	Rededication	Other	Total
1–10	74%	8%	4%	14%	100%
11–13	68%	13%	8%	11%	100%
14–18	58%	16%	14%	12%	100%
19–25	50%	16%	20%	14%	100%
26–39	47%	15%	25%	13%	100%
40–59	46%	15%	26%	13%	100%
60 and over	44%	16%	26%	14%	100%
Overall	56%	14%	17%	13%	100%

(N = 78,936)

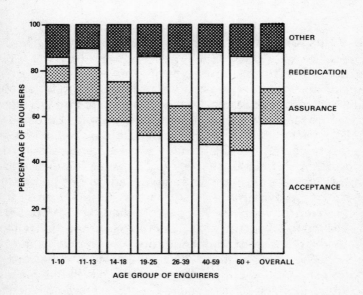

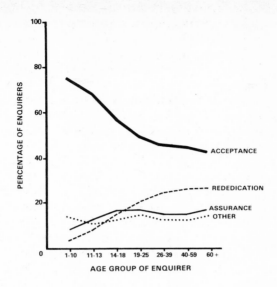

Table 13: Summary of response — adults and children

Percentage of enquirers

Age-group	Acceptance	Assurance	Rededication	Other	Total
18 and under	64%	14%	10%	12%	100%
Over 18	47%	15%	24%	14%	100%

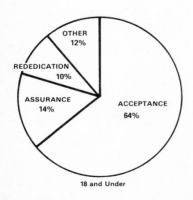

39

Returning to the more detailed breakdown in Table 12, it can be seen that the proportion of enquirers seeking to accept Christ is extremely high— almost three quarters of the total — amongst younger children, and reduces steadily with increasing age. This is counterbalanced by a very low proportion of child enquirers wishing to rededicate themselves, a proportion which increases steadily with age. Similarly, a smaller than average proportion of children going forward were seeking assurance of salvation, whilst the proportion of adults responding in this way is higher; this however does not seem to vary with age amongst the adults.

The higher proportion of children and young people making a first commitment no doubt reflects the smaller numbers of previously committed Christians in this age-group. The increasing incidence of rededication in older age-groups confirms that many people have in the past responded to the challenge, but have subsequently failed to maintain their commitment in later life. A relatively small proportion of children required assurance about their salvation, but the proportions of teenagers and adults are relatively consistent. These figures suggest strongly that there are large numbers of people in society who have had some form of spiritual experience in the past, but who remain uncertain about the validity of their commitment and its relevance to their everyday lives. The Church must present itself to such people as an organism which is able to respond to these needs through Christian teaching and caring. Failure to do this could mean that many of those who went forward for the first time at Mission England will in a few years be as lost to the Church as their predecessors.

The proportions going forward for other reasons do not vary particularly with age, although they are lowest amongst teenagers. Does this perhaps reflect a tendency amongst this age-group to perceive the issues with more clarity and a need to respond definitively to a direct personal challenge?

Emphasis has so far been placed on the varying responses of different age-groups, and it is therefore worth pointing out that the overriding response of all age-groups is the desire to know Jesus as personal Saviour.

Generally speaking, the national pattern is reflected in the figures for each of the local missions, and for the most part those differences that do arise can be accounted for in terms of the particular character of the Mission as set out in Table 11. Comment in this respect on the local missions will therefore be confined to the most noteworthy features.

Table 11 suggested that the missions at Bristol, Norwich and Ipswich saw a greater response from individuals with previous Christian commitment than was the case at the other missions. At Bristol this was a feature of all age-groups but was particularly marked among enquirers over 60 years of age; 47% sought either assurance or rededication as against 42% nationally. At Norwich, the difference in response among those over 60 was even more dramatic with 53% seeking assurance or rededication, and only 33% responding by accepting Christ as against 44% nationally. There was also a higher than expected proportion of enquirers in the 26–39 age-group at Norwich who sought to rededicate themselves, whilst at Ipswich a similar unexpectedly high proportion rededicating themselves was observed among the 19–25 age-group. The increased incidence of rededication among those of later years may reflect a greater degree of spirituality in the nation in the past, but the figures for young adults in East Anglia suggest that these groups have been successfully reached in their youth and failed to maintain a depth of commitment in adulthood.

At Birmingham, on the other hand, the striking feature is the relatively high incidence of first-time commitment among adult enquirers, which does not decrease with age as would be expected. Nearly half of those aged 26 or over responded in this way and the difference between the Birmingham figure and the national picture is particularly marked among the over 60's, 48% of whom accepted Christ as Saviour as against 44% nationwide. This figure contrasts vividly with the 33% of over 60's at Norwich who responded by acceptance; it also serves to illustrate the difference between the two missions: the one strongly evangelistic and challenging the uncommitted, the other a call to renew and revitalise a faith once expressed but subsequently neglected.

The figures from Liverpool and Sunderland are closest overall to the national response pattern and there are in fact no exceptional features in the response of different age-groups at Liverpool. At Sunderland, however, there is an interesting difference in the responses of young people on the one hand and adults on the other. Above average percentages of young enquirers wished to make a first commitment to Christ, whilst the proportion of adults rededicating themselves is also above average and particularly so among those aged 40 and over. Does this suggest a wider spiritual 'generation gap' than elsewhere in the country, or is it that young people in the area were more successful in inviting unsaved friends?

Type of response and sex of enquirer

To what extent did the type of response made by enquirers vary according to their sex? Table 14 shows that over Mission England as a whole the difference in response between the sexes was relatively small.

Table 14: Type of response and sex of enquirer

		Acceptance	Assurance	Rededication	Other	Total
			Percentage responding by			
Bristol	Male	56%	14%	17%	13%	100%
	Female	53%	14%	20%	13%	100%
Sunderland	Male	57%	13%	17%	13%	100%
	Female	55%	14%	19%	12%	100%
Norwich	Male	51%	15%	20%	14%	100%
	Female	49%	18%	20%	13%	100%
B'ham	Male	57%	15%	14%	14%	100%
	Female	56%	16%	15%	13%	100%
Liverpool	Male	57%	13%	15%	15%	100%
	Female	55%	13%	18%	14%	100%
Ipswich	Male	57%	15%	15%	13%	100%
	Female	52%	16%	19%	13%	100%
Overall	Male	57%	14%	16%	13%	100%
	Female	55%	14%	18%	13%	100%

(N=82,376)

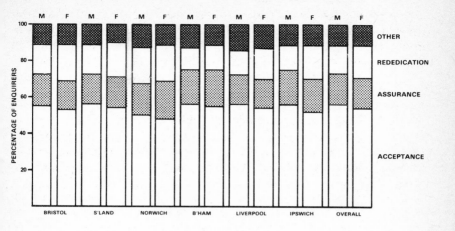

In general, the proportion of male enquirers who wished to accept Christ was slightly higher than the corresponding female enquirers, whilst the proportion of females who wished to rededicate themselves was generally higher than was the case for men. The proportions seeking assurance of salvation, or responding for other reasons, were virtually identical between the sexes. This suggests that a higher proportion of the women who responded at Mission England had already made some previous form of commitment, but the difference is not greatly marked. These figures confirm that there is little difference between the sexes in terms of spiritual needs.

The overall picture is generally reflected in the area missions, with a higher proportion of male enquirers seeking to accept Christ being a consistent feature at each venue — including Norwich, where although the proportions themselves are lower, the pattern is similar. As regards the proportions seeking to rededicate themselves, the higher proportion of female enquirers generally is also seen at all venues other than Norwich, where in fact the proportions in this respect are identical. At Norwich, the principal difference between the sexes appears to have arisen in connection with assurance of salvation, where the proportion of females who required counselling in this respect differed from the male percentage by a wider margin than was generally the case elsewhere.

The only other significant feature of the figures at individual missions arises at Ipswich, where the differences between the sexes in the proportions accepting Christ are much more marked than at other venues. At this mission, it would seem that the proportion of men responding for the first time was similar to the large urban missions, whilst a greater degree of prior commitment was encountered amongst female enquirers.

Type of Response by Occupational Grouping

The counsellor forms allowed for the recording of the occupation of the enquirer, although unfortunately the classifications used do not

Table 15: Type of Response by Occupational Group

	Acceptance	Assurance	Rededication	Other	Total
Agricultural	45%	16%	23%	16%	100%
Armed Forces	45%	11%	31%	13%	100%
Civil Servants	45%	15%	25%	15%	100%
Clerical workers	47%	15%	25%	13%	100%
Finance	49%	17%	22%	12%	100%
Homemakers	47%	15%	25%	13%	100%
Industrial workers	53%	15%	20%	12%	100%
Management	42%	13%	29%	16%	100%
Medical	44%	17%	26%	13%	100%
Professional	43%	16%	29%	12%	100%
Religious	14%	9%	58%	19%	100%
Students	64%	14%	11%	11%	100%
Teachers	33%	15%	36%	16%	100%
Transport workers	52%	14%	19%	15%	100%
Wholesale/Retail	53%	14%	21%	12%	100%
Unemployed	54%	14%	17%	15%	100%
Other	47%	15%	23%	15%	100%
Overall	56%	14%	17%	13%	100%
Overall excluding students	48%	15%	23%	14%	100%

(N = 81,896)

Type of Response by Occupational Group

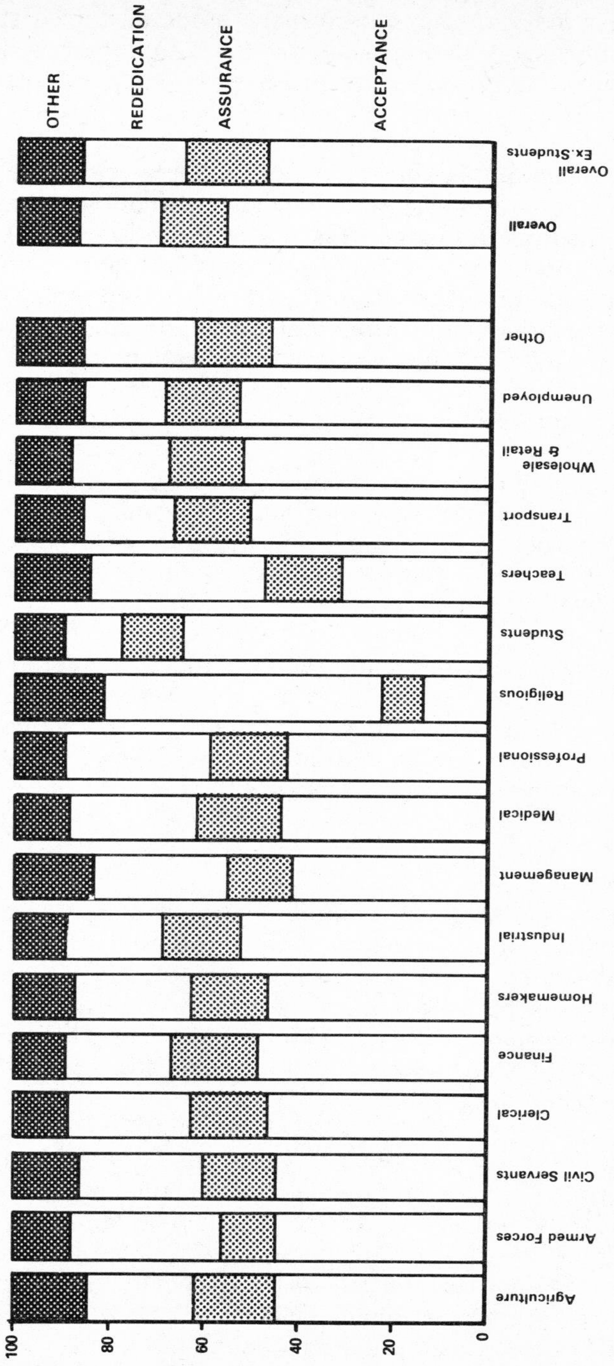

readily allow us to apportion these amongst the socio-economic groupings used by the Government. The various classifications used and the types of responses made by each occupational group are shown in Table 15.

It is not altogether surprising that the highest incidence of enquirers accepting Christ as Saviour occurred amongst those describing themselves as students. This group were predominantly young people, and it has already been observed that the overwhelming majority of young people going forward responded in this way. Considerations of age rather than occupational characteristics also account for the low incidence of rededication amongst this group; the level of previous religious commitment will inevitably be lower amongst the young.

Almost half of the total number of respondents at Mission England described themselves as students, and it may therefore be more instructive to compare the response of other occupational groups with the response of non-students generally, which is also shown in the table.

Other occupational groups with a higher than average proportion of enquirers wishing to accept Christ include the unemployed, which may again be a reflection of the high level of unemployment amongst young people in Britain today. Other groups where over 50% of those going forward accepted Christ as Saviour were industrial workers, those employed in the wholesale and retail trades, and transport workers.

The lowest incidence of individuals accepting Christ as Saviour occurred amongst those working in the religious field, which includes not only ministers and priests but also full-time Christian workers and nuns. It is hardly surprising that the majority of the fairly small number who responded in this category sought to rededicate themselves, although there were some who made a first commitment to Christ.

A fascinating figure which is less readily explained is the low proportion of those employed in the teaching profession who went forward to accept Christ. Apart from the religious classification, this is the only occupational grouping where the proportion wishing to rededicate themselves exceeds those seeking to make a first commitment, and we can only speculate as to why this should be so. Does it reflect a greater degree of religious experience amongst the teaching profession, or is it the manifestation of a greater degree of scepticism leading to a higher than average proportion of enquirers with a prior commitment?

A lower than average proportion of enquirers accepting Christ is also seen in the management and professional categories, where again the proportion of enquirers seeking to rededicate themselves is above average. This result tends to confirm the suggestion that prior religious experience is more prevalent amongst those of higher socio-economic standing. Further indication of this is given by the low proportion of enquirers seeking rededication amongst industrial workers, transport workers and those employed in the wholesale and retail trades.

It is interesting to note that the proportion seeking assurance of salvation does not, with one or two exceptions, vary widely according to occupational classification; doubt and uncertainty are factors which affect all echelons of society. It is perhaps not surprising that the lowest proportion of those requiring assurance arose in the religious category, where one would suppose the individuals concerned have a deeper understanding of such things than their secular counterparts. Of rather more interest, therefore, is the low proportion of enquirers from the armed forces who responded in this way. Perhaps the nature of their employment allows less room for uncertainty in these matters. Certainly this group shows an exceptionally high proportion of individuals who responded by rededication, suggesting again that religious commitment is difficult to maintain in the Forces environment.

Apart from those employed in the religious sphere, the proportions responding for other reasons are fairly consistent across all occupational groups.

As regards the pattern at individual missions, this appears to be broadly similar for most of the major occupational groups. Such differences as do arise appear generally to reflect the particular character of each of the local missions, which has already been discussed, rather than any peculiar characteristics of occupational groups in that locality.

Type of Response and Denominational Background

How significant was the denominational origin of an enquirer in determining the type of response that was made? Clearly, a large

Table 16: Type of response and denominational background — national

	Acceptance	Assurance	Rededication	Other	Total
African/ W Indian	53%	17%	14%	16%	100%
Anglican	55%	14%	18%	13%	100%
Baptist	59%	14%	14%	13%	100%
Independent	61%	13%	14%	12%	100%
Methodist	56%	15%	17%	12%	100%
Pentecostal	57%	14%	16%	13%	100%
Roman Catholic	47%	15%	22%	16%	100%
Salvation Army	42%	18%	31%	9%	100%
URC/ Congregational	55%	14%	18%	13%	100%
Other	58%	14%	15%	13%	100%
Overall	56%	14%	17%	13%	100% (N=78,359)

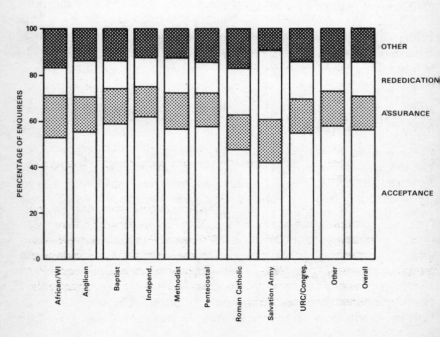

48

number of enquirers would have had only the most tenuous of links with any denomination, but just over 80% of enquirers were able to provide some form of response to this question. The number who claimed no denominational link was actually quite small, but this should not be taken as indicative that most of those who went forward had established church links.

The types of response given by enquirers from different denominations are shown in the table opposite. Some clarification is perhaps needed as to what denominations each of these groupings embraces. The 'Independent' churches include FIEC churches, Brethren assemblies and House Churches. 'URC/Congregational' includes all Presbyterian churches, whilst the 'Other' category includes smaller Christian groups and also all non-Christian religions and sects.

Of those who responded 45% claimed an association with the Anglican church, although many of these were far from regular attenders. Given the preponderance of this denominational background over any other, it is not surprising that the response pattern for Anglicans is similar to that seen over the whole range of responses, with 55% of enquirers going forward to accept Christ, 14% to receive assurance of salvation, 18% to rededicate themselves, and 13% for other reasons.

The highest proportion of enquirers who wished to accept Christ arose among those from an Independent church background. This is interesting, since these churches generally claim an evangelical tradition, and the number of individuals with looser association would tend to be much smaller than in the major denominations. Similarly high proportions of those accepting Christ occurred in those claiming a Baptist association, where again there is an evangelical emphasis. Do these figures perhaps reflect the sowing of seeds during regular church activities which bore fruit in the Mission England arenas?

The figures in respect of the Salvation Army and the Roman Catholics are vastly different. Only 42% of Salvationists who went forward did so to accept Christ, but 31% went forward for rededication, by far the largest percentage for any of the denominational groupings. In addition, 18% of the Salvationists who responded were uncertain of their salvation, again the highest percentage for any of the denominational groups.

Among the Roman Catholics nearly half responded by accepting the message of salvation, but again a high percentage wished to rededicate themselves.

These figures for the Salvation Army and the Roman Catholics suggest either a lack of depth in prior commitment or a failure to live this out in daily life.

Amongst those seeking assurance of salvation, the proportion is highest among those with Salvation Army or African/West Indian church links.

The lowest percentages of enquirers wishing to rededicate themselves occurred in the Baptist, Independent and African/West Indian groups, suggesting that those who associate themselves with these churches have a greater depth of commitment. Associations with churches in these traditions tend to be less nominal, and there is therefore a greater encouragement towards a growing faith than is perhaps the case in the other denominational groupings generally.

Notwithstanding these remarks, the figures also demonstrate graphically the common need of all of us, irrespective of denominational origin or affiliation, to find a Saviour and a practical faith for everyday living.

At the local level, the figures for each of the Missions represent quite closely the national denominational picture in conjunction with the pattern of response demonstrated in Table 11. The widest differences arise in smaller denominations where the numbers involved do not allow for firm conclusions.

It is nevertheless interesting to note that at Norwich, while most denominations showed a lower incidence of enquirers accepting Christ, the proportion of such enquirers from an Independent church background was very much more in line with the national average. Three-fifths of these enquirers sought to accept Christ, as against 50% overall at this mission. Does this indicate that contacts made by these churches were with individuals outside the Church, whilst other denominations were experiencing a greater renewal of commitment and a lesser degree of conversion growth?

The response made by those with URC/Congregational links was also interesting in that, at Sunderland, a larger than expected proportion wished to rededicate themselves whilst in contrast at Liverpool nearly two-thirds went forward to receive Christ, as against 55% nationally.

CHARACTERISTICS OF ENQUIRERS

Introduction

We have already examined the responsiveness of people attending Mission England, and the ways in which individuals responded. The information on the counsellor forms can also be used to provide us with a profile of who the enquirers actually were, and in this section we shall be concentrating on particular characteristics of the enquirers, both in the nation as a whole and also at each of the six area missions.

Age

Age has emerged as a very significant factor in determining the type of response made by enquirers. So just how old were those who went forward at Mission England? Table 17 below sets out the percentage of enquirers for each of the age-groups and compares this with the percentage represented by this age-group of the general population of England and Wales. (It has been assumed for this purpose that none of the enquirers was aged five or under.)

Table 17: Age of enquirers

Age-group	Mission England enquirers	General population
10 and under	9%	8%
11–13	18%	6%
14–18	27%	8%
19–25	11%	11%
26–39	15%	20%
40–59	15%	25%
60 and over	5%	22%
N (=100%)	78,936	44.8m

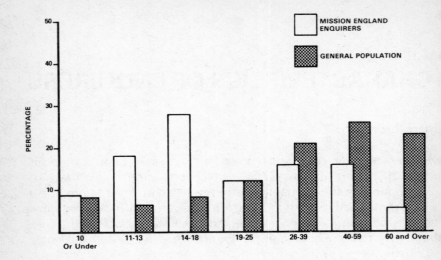

People of all ages responded, although in varying degrees, indicating that there was a message for everyone who attended Mission England.

It is most noticeable, nevertheless, that the outstanding response came from those in younger age-groups. The contrast between under 18's and adults is seen even more clearly from the summary in Table 18.

Over half the total number of people who went forward at Mission England were aged 18 or under. The figures are evidently in stark contrast to the proportions of the total population represented by these age-groups.

Table 18: Age of enquirers — summary

Age-group	Mission England enquirers	General population
18 and under	54%	22%
Over 18	46%	78%

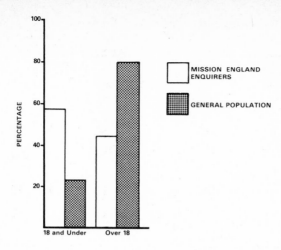

MISSION ENGLAND
ENQUIRERS

GENERAL POPULATION

Looking at the response from young people in more detail, it is noted that the proportion of children aged 10 and under who responded is more or less what we would expect from the proportion of this age-group in the general population. Amongst young teenagers, however, the response is nearly three times as great as the proportion of the population, and this figure is exceeded still further by the response from older teenagers. These figures confirm that the young are seekers after truth, and the evangelistic emphasis in our churches should recognise the high level of responsiveness among teenagers, which is significantly greater than amongst older age-groups. One of the lessons to be learned from Mission England is that young people today still find the gospel message relevant to their personal circumstances, and will respond to an adequately presented challenge.

It is interesting that the proportion of enquirers from the 19–25 age-group is similar to the proportion that this group represents of the population. Above this age-group, however, the proportions of enquirers fall below the numbers in the population as a whole. 35% of those who went forward were over 26 years of age, as against two-thirds of the population.

Nevertheless, the numbers of enquirers in the 40–59 age-group, which constituted 15% of Mission England enquirers, is higher than might have been expected. The people in this age-group are, of course, the young of the 1950's, and it is tempting to think that the increased responsiveness of these people was due to a reawakening of commitment made during much earlier Billy Graham

55

crusades. It will be recalled from the previous analysis that the incidence of rededication amongst individuals from this age-group was
significantly higher than among those of younger years.

The table below shows the ages of enquirers at each of the local
missions:

Table 19: Age of enquirers at local missions

Age-group	Bristol	S'land	Norwich	B'ham	L'pool	Ipswich	Overall
10 or under	7%	9%	9%	9%	8%	12%	9%
11–13	20%	18%	20%	17%	17%	18%	18%
14–18	31%	28%	22%	27%	26%	22%	27%
19–25	11%	11%	11%	11%	11%	11%	11%
26–39	14%	14%	17%	15%	16%	17%	15%
40–59	13%	15%	15%	16%	16%	15%	15%
60 and over	4%	5%	6%	5%	6%	5%	5%
N (= 100%)	13,788	11,043	3,369	22,619	22,086	6,031	78,936

There are some interesting variations here, particularly as regards the teenagers who responded. 51% of those who responded
at Bristol were under 13 as against 45% in Mission England as a
whole, whilst in contrast at Ipswich only 40% were teenagers, and at
Norwich only 42%; these areas contain similar proportions of
young people as a percentage of their overall population. These
figures are offset by a lower than average percentage of older
people going forward at Bristol, and a higher than average response
from these age-groups at the East Anglian missions, although it is
noticeable that at Ipswich the proportion of child enquirers was substantially greater than anything seen elsewhere.

It is also interesting that the proportion of enquirers in the 19–25
age-group hardly varies at all across the nation, and corresponds almost exactly to the proportion that this group bears to the general
population as a whole.

Age-groups of enquirers at local missions

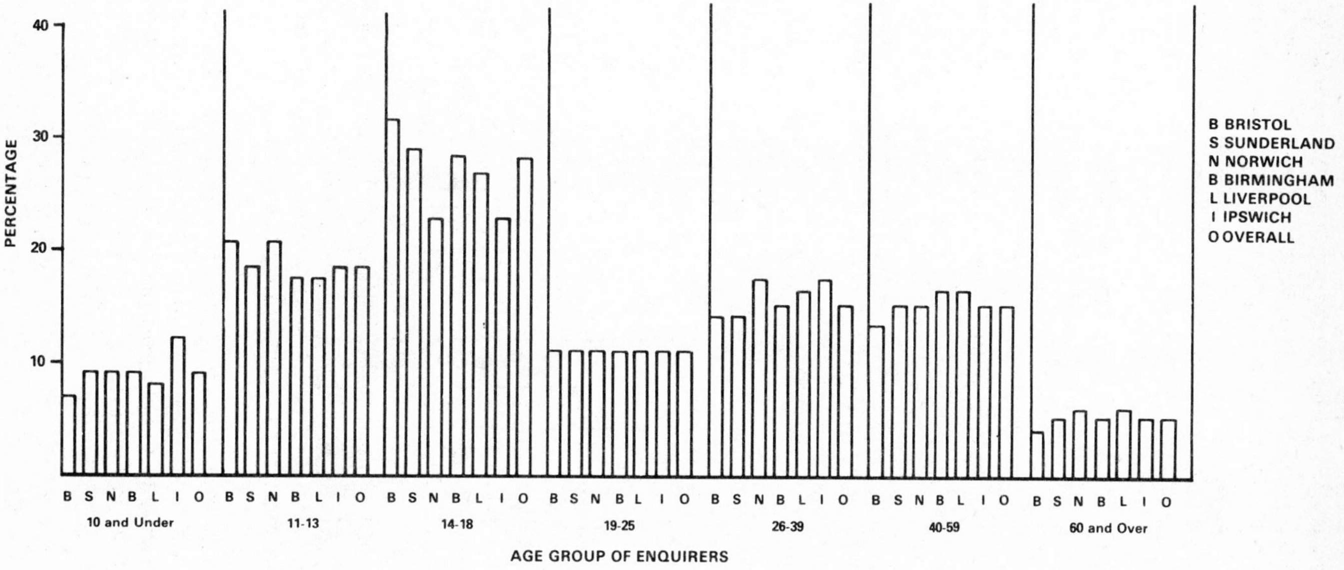

B BRISTOL
S SUNDERLAND
N NORWICH
B BIRMINGHAM
L LIVERPOOL
I IPSWICH
O OVERALL

PERCENTAGE

AGE GROUP OF ENQUIRERS

B S N B L I O   10 and Under
B S N B L I O   11-13
B S N B L I O   14-18
B S N B L I O   19-25
B S N B L I O   26-39
B S N B L I O   40-59
B S N B L I O   60 and Over

40
30
20
10

57

In the following table, the numbers of people making specific types of response are broken down between the age-groups:

Table 20: Ages of those making specific responses (national)

Age-group	Acceptance	Assurance	Rededication	Other	Overall
10 and under	11%	5%	2%	9%	9%
11–13	22%	15%	8%	15%	18%
14–18	28%	30%	22%	26%	27%
19–25	10%	12%	13%	12%	11%
26–39	13%	16%	23%	16%	15%
40–59	12%	16%	24%	16%	15%
60 and over	4%	6%	8%	6%	5%
N (=100%)	44,156	11,320	13,270	10,190	78,936

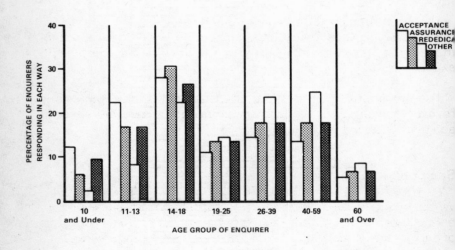

Of those who went forward with the express purpose of accepting Christ as Saviour, the overwhelming majority were under the age of 18, and indeed, 50% were teenagers. Nevertheless, the table shows that people of all ages did respond in this way, and 4% of those making a first-time commitment — just over 1,800 people — were 60 years of age or older.

58

The need for assurance of salvation is also a feature of all age-groups, with the possible exception of children who appear to have less uncertainty in this area. Half of those who went forward for this reason were aged over 19, and whilst many of these are probably not regular attenders at church, the need for clear teaching on this subject to counter the nominalism in society today is quite apparent.

The majority of those rededicating themselves were aged over 26, and in fact 55% of those responding in this way came from these age-groups. People in this part of the age scale are, of course, much more likely to have had a prior spiritual experience, and in such circumstances rededication is obviously the appropriate response. Nevertheless, 30% of those who responded in this way were teenagers, which perhaps is a comment on the difficulty that many of today's young people find in maintaining their Christian commitment in everyday life. As one might expect, the proportion of those responding in this way who were children is very small indeed, whilst the 60 and over age-group represents 8% of those going forward for this reason, as against only 5% overall.

The proportions responding for other reasons tend to correspond quite closely to the overall response patterns, with the exception of those in the 11–13 age-group where the figure is less than we might expect.

The breakdown of these figures for each of the local missions reveals few variations that are not explained by the differences in age distribution already outlined.

Sex of enquirers

We have already examined the types of response made by members of the different sexes, but have not established the proportions of each of the sexes in the total number of those going forward.

These figures are set out in Table 21, from which it may be seen that female enquirers outnumbered males by just over three to two. The proportions are similar at each of the area missions, although at Ipswich the proportion of female enquirers was a little lower than at any other venue. The lowest proportion of male enquirers occurred at Sunderland.

Table 21: Sex of enquirers (national and local)

	Male	Female	
Bristol	37%	63%	
Sunderland	35%	65%	
Norwich	36%	64%	
Birmingham	37%	63%	
Liverpool	37%	63%	
Ipswich	40%	60%	
Overall	37%	63%	(N = 82,376)

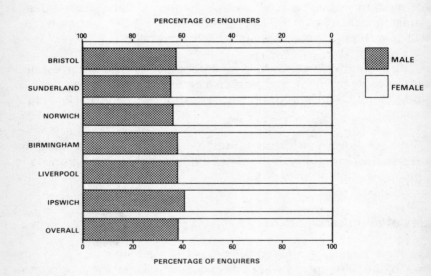

Sex and age

The figures shown above do, nevertheless, conceal some disparity in the different age-groups, as is evidenced by the following table:

60

Table 22: Sex of enquirers by age-group (national)

Age-group	Male	Female	Total
10 and under	44%	56%	100%
11–13	41%	59%	100%
14–18	40%	60%	100%
19–25	42%	58%	100%
26–39	33%	67%	100%
40–59	30%	70%	100%
60 and over	26%	74%	100%.
Overall	37%	63%	100%

(N = 78,829)

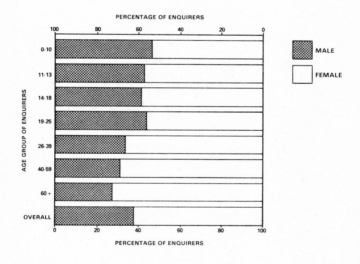

Whilst females are in the majority in each age-group, there is a wide variation between the sexes. The proportion of men generally reduces as age increases; the same pattern is apparent in church attendance across the nation. The difference between the sexes is relatively narrow among the youngest children, but in those aged 60 and over there are three female enquirers for every man. These figures are disproportionate to the sex distribution of the population as a whole.

61

What is it, then, which causes men over the age of 25 to be so re-
luctant to come forward? Were the organisers successful in per-
suading this age-group even to attend the Mission? Is it peer pressure, or a feeling that 'religion is for women and children'?

The following table shows the proportion of the total number of
enquirers represented by each sex/age-group combination.

Table 23: Sex of enquirers and age-group (national)

Age-group	Mission England enquirers			General Population		
	Male	Female	Total	Male	Female	Total
10 and under	4%	5%	9%	7%	6%	13%
11–13	7%	11%	18%	2%	2%	4%
14–18	11%	16%	27%	4%	4%	8%
19–25	5%	6%	11%	5%	5%	10%
26–39	5%	10%	15%	10%	10%	20%
40–59%	4%	11%	15%	12%	12%	24%
60 and over	1%	4%	5%	9%	12%	21%
Total	37%	63%	100%	49%	51%	100%
		(N=78,829)			(N=48.5m)	

The largest single group by far are girls in the 14–18 age-group.
The next largest groups in numerical terms are girls between 11 and
13, boys in the 14–18 age-group, and women aged between 40 and
59; these groups together represent half of all those who went forward. The smallest group, again by some way, are men over the age
of 60. This group represents considerably more than 1% of the
population as a whole, and the figures for men over the age of 19
generally fall well short of the proportions these age-groups actually represent in the general population. It is felt that these figures
demonstrate dramatically the relative lack of impact of Mission England amongst adult males.

Occupation

What were the occupations of those who came forward? The counsellor form allowed for 16 categories of occupation, including
'unemployed', and an additional category for those whose occupation

Sex of enquirers and age-group (national)

did not conveniently fit into one of the classifications. The 'other' category includes, but is by no means limited to, retired people. The following table shows the numbers who responded in each occupational classification, and the proportion that each group represents of the total response. The three smallest groups are too small to show up in the table, but when the figures for each of these are added, they make up the 1% which is not accounted for elsewhere.

Table 24: Occupation of enquirers

Occupation	Proportion
Students	49%
Homemakers	13%
Unemployed	5%
Industrial	5%
Clerical	4%
Medical	3%
Wholesale/Retail	3%
Teaching	2%
Others	16%
N (=100%)	87,925

Very nearly half of the total number who went forward gave their occupation as 'student', which includes schoolchildren. The next largest group were homemakers (this term is used rather than 'housewives' because 59 men described themselves in this category), who represented 13% of the total. It is a sad reflection on the times in which we live that the third largest occupational group, representing 5% of the respondents, were unemployed; industria workers accounted for a similar but slightly smaller percentage.

Although the overwhelming response came from students, this table does indicate that there was a message for everyone in what was preached at Mission England. People from varying backgrounds responded to the challenge: schoolchildren and teachers, managers and industrial workers, professional people and typists; in all, the self-employed, employees and indeed, the unemployed. Each found the gospel relevant to their particular circumstances.

Occupation and sex

Despite the pressure for equality between the sexes, most occupational groups still show a strong sexual bias, which is equally evident in the breakdown of enquirers' occupations by sex. The 17 classifications used would make a detailed breakdown cumbersome and of limited value, but Table 25 indicates the largest occupational groups by sex.

Students predominate in both sexes, accounting for over half of the male enquirers and just under half of the females. The next largest occupational group amongst men is the industrial workers, representing one in ten of the men who went forward, with the unemployed also prominent; 1 in 11 of the men who responded at Mission England was unemployed.

Table 25: Occupation of enquirers by sex:
largest occupational groups (national)

Male enquirers:	Students	54%
	Industrial	10%
	Unemployed	9%
Female enquirers:	Students	46%
	Homemakers	20%
	Clerical	5%
All enquirers	Students	49%
	Homemakers	13%
	Unemployed	5%

65

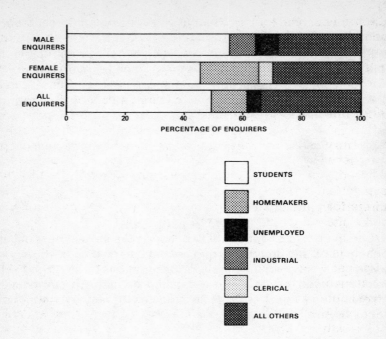

Amongst women, 1 in 5 described themselves as a homemaker or housewife, and altogether students and homemakers account for nearly two-thirds of the women who responded. The next largest occupational group, with 5% of the total female response, are clerical workers.

At the local missions similar characteristics emerged. Students, not unexpectedly, predominated everywhere but particularly at Bristol where they represented 56% of all enquirers as against just under half nationally. At Liverpool 1 in 8 of the male enquirers and 1 in 12 of all enquirers were unemployed, a substantially higher percentage than at other venues.

Occupation and age

Perhaps the most interesting figures here relate to the unemployed. 6% of respondents in the 14–18 age-group were unemployed, which means that one-third of the non-students who responded from this age-group are at present without a job. Of those who responded in the 19–25 age-group 16% were also in this position, and unemployed people from each age-group responded in some measure to Dr Graham's message of hope. This group represents approximately 9% of those enquirers who were of working age, a little less than the proportion of unemployed people in the working-age population.

Denomination of enquirers

Enquirers were asked to indicate their denominational background, and most were able to do this. The degree of association was not established, and for many enquirers the link with a church will have been extremely tenuous. Table 26 indicates the percentage of enquirers for each denominational group, and compares this with church attendance in England (1979 figures).

There is a considerable disparity between the percentages of enquirers at Mission England and the figures for those attending church generally. Anglicans represent only one-third of church attenders, but accounted for nearly half of the enquirers at Mission England. Anglican enquirers at the missions will have included people with established church links, but many of those who rarely attend church also describe themselves as 'C of E', and the response from this group would give rise to the increased Anglican proportion that is evident here.

Table 26: Denominational background of enquirers (national)

	Total enquirers	National church attendance
Anglican	46%	33%
Baptist	12%	5%
Independent	8%	5%
Methodist	13%	12%
Pentecostal	6%	2%
Roman Catholic	6%	34%
URC/Congregational	3%	4%
African/W Indian	0%	}
Salvation Army	1%	5%
Other	5%	
N (=100%)	84,137	3.9 million

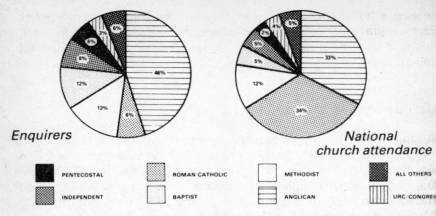

Enquirers

National
church attendance

■ PENTECOSTAL	▨ ROMAN CATHOLIC	☐ METHODIST	▨ ALL OTHERS
▨ INDEPENDENT	☐ BAPTIST	☰ ANGLICAN	▥ URC/CONGRE

The response amongst Roman Catholics stands in complete contrast. These also account for around one-third of church attendance, but only 6% of Mission England enquirers came from a Catholic background. These figures lead us to ask whether Catholic support for the Mission was sufficiently positive at the local church level.

Amongst other denominational groups, it is noticeable that the proportion of enquirers from Baptist, Independent and Pentecostal backgrounds is in each case somewhat greater than in the church attendance figures for these groups. These churches generally tend to be more evangelical in their outlook, and the figures indicate that they were successful in bringing those with spiritual needs to the missions. Was it that they promoted the Mission more effectively, or do the statistics reflect the activity of individual members in inviting unsaved friends? To what extent do the figures reflect seeds sown through prolonged contact with these churches?

Table 27 shows the breakdown of these figures by each of the local missions. Enquirers from Anglican backgrounds predominated at all venues, but particularly at Norwich. A substantially smaller proportion at Sunderland claimed Anglican association, however, and the compensating factor was the substantially above average proportion of Methodist enquirers in the north-east. Methodists were much less prominent at Bristol and Ipswich. Baptists were evidently out in force at Bristol and Ipswich, but were relatively poorly represented among Liverpool enquirers. Here the Catholic response was much greater than anywhere else, due no doubt to the greater numbers of Catholics in the area, and in stark contrast to the very poor response from Catholics at Birmingham. A similar disparity is evident among the Pentecostals, whose strong presence among Birmingham enquirers is out of all proportion to

68

response from this group at the missions and particularly those in East Anglia.

Table 27: Denominational background of enquirers (local)

	Bristol	S'land	Norwich	B'ham	L'pool	Ipswich	Overall
African/ W Indian	0%	0%	0%	1%	0%	0%	0%
Anglican	46%	39%	55%	43%	50%	48%	46%
Baptist	16%	9%	10%	14%	6%	16%	12%
Independent	9%	6%	7%	8%	10%	8%	8%
Methodist	9%	21%	10%	13%	12%	8%	13%
Pentecostal	5%	6%	2%	11%	4%	3%	6%
R. Catholic	4%	8%	4%	1%	11%	4%	6%
Salvn. Army	1%	2%	2%	1%	1%	1%	1%
URC/Congr.	3%	3%	2%	2%	4%	4%	3%
Other	7%	6%	8%	5%	2%	8%	5%
N (= 100%)	18,880	11,542	3,478	21,226	22,778	6,433	84,137

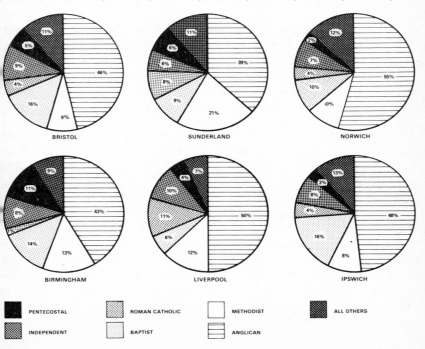

PENTECOSTAL   ROMAN CATHOLIC   METHODIST   ALL OTHERS

INDEPENDENT   BAPTIST   ANGLICAN

Denomination and occupation

There were seventeen occupational classifications, and to reproduce the full statistics for this area would be counter-productive. We have therefore selected the three largest identified occupational groups, together with two other groups with unusual characteristics, for inclusion in the table below.

Among the larger occupational groups, the widest disparity was amongst the unemployed. Here, only 37% of enquirers claimed Anglican association, whilst the proportions from Independent and Pentecostal church backgrounds were much higher than the overall average. Have these churches been more successful in reaching the unemployed?

The response pattern from the teaching fraternity was unusual, and the denominational characteristics of this group are equally unexpected. A much higher than average proportion were Anglican or Roman Catholic, whilst the proportion of teachers from Baptist, Independent and Pentecostal backgrounds was well below the national average. It will be recalled that a larger than average

Table 28: Denominational background of selected occupational groups

	Students	Homemkrs	Unempl	Teachers	Forces	Overall
Afr/W Indian	0%	0%	1%	0%	0%	0%
Anglican	44%	50%	37%	59%	33%	46%
Baptist	13%	10%	13%	8%	15%	12%
Independent	9%	7%	11%	4%	6%	8%
Methodist	14%	12%	10%	11%	11%	13%
Pentecostal	5%	6%	10%	2%	6%	6%
R. Catholic	5%	7%	8%	10%	8%	6%
Salvn. Army	1%	1%	1%	0%	0%	1%
URC/Congr.	3%	3%	3%	4%	3%	3%
Other	6%	4%	6%	2%	18%	5%
N (=100%)	41,225	10,735	4,537	1,284	200	83,601

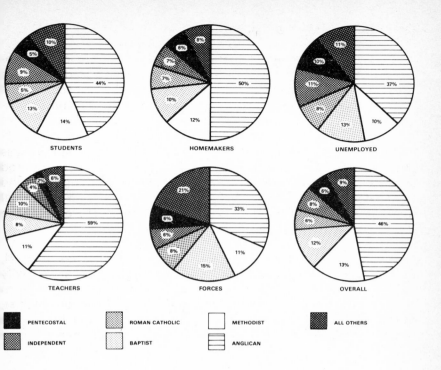

STUDENTS HOMEMAKERS UNEMPLOYED

TEACHERS FORCES OVERALL

PENTECOSTAL   ROMAN CATHOLIC   METHODIST   ALL OTHERS

INDEPENDENT   BAPTIST   ANGLICAN

proportion of these responded by rededication. The message of these figures is not clear; are teachers more attracted by traditional denominations, and if so, why should this be?

The number responding from the armed forces is small, and it is dangerous therefore to read too much into the figures. What is evident, however, is that a very low proportion — only about one-third — of all forces enquirers consider themselves Anglicans, whilst no less than 18% were unable to give themselves a denominational label. Part of the explanation may be a tendency for Christians in this employment to attend interdenominational churches at their camps.

Generally, the denominational backgrounds of those from other occupational groups were not exceptional.

GEOGRAPHICAL PATTERNS OF ATTENDANCE

It is not, in fact, possible to determine precisely where the people who attended Mission England came from, simply because no survey was taken of those coming to the meetings. We may, nevertheless, be able to draw some tentative conclusions from the information which was obtained about enquirers, which included in most cases details of their address. Such information is, naturally, highly confidential, and that confidence must be respected; nevertheless, it is possible to examine the outer or district element of the postcode without betraying personal secrets. A small team therefore spent a considerable length of time organising postcodes into coherent statistics and accumulating totals for each postcode district; altogether some 86,317 postcodes were examined in this way.

A typical British postcode is BR8 7JE; the outer element used in this analysis would be the 'BR8' part. There are in total some 2,700 such elements covering on average 8,300 addresses each. A high degree of anonymity is thus preserved.

Whilst we can be fairly confident that the enquirers' origins are representative of the attendance as a whole, we ought for the sake of balance to mention the possible elements of bias which could distort the true picture. In the first place, it will be observed that something over 10,000 of the total number of enquirers — approximately 1% — were unable to provide a postcode or an address from which a postcode could be determined, or provided information which was later found to be incorrect. The proportion of missing postcodes varied widely across the six missions, and particular attention is drawn to it where it could be a significant element in interpretation of the results. It must be assumed, however, that there is no degree of bias in the failure to provide this information; in other words, that ignorance of the postcode is a factor which affects all sections of the population, irrespective of economic status or geographical origin.

Secondly, and perhaps more importantly, we have also had to

73

assume for the purpose of this analysis that the gospel appeals equally to all sectors of the population irrespective of the area in which they live, which may in turn be influenced by their economic status.

This type of analysis is extremely useful, as it enables us to assess those areas from which people were originally drawn to Mission England, which directions they travelled from, and in each case the distance that people were prepared to travel to hear Billy Graham's message. It thus helps to define the character of a mission — was it really an 'Area' mission, or was the attendance composed of the immediate population? This analysis is not only useful in evaluating the impact of a mission that has taken place, but can also be used to provide a basis for planning of similar future events.

In the paragraphs which follow, each of the area missions is assessed independently, following which some overall conclusions are drawn. For each of the missions, a stylised map is presented indicating the three regions into which the area has been divided. These approximate to the immediate urban area, an area of approximately 15 miles' radius from the city centre, and a further area of approximtely 30 miles' range from the centre. These have been designated as 'central', 'inner', and 'outer'. The inner and outer areas have been further subdivided into north, south, east and west. The intricacies of the British postcode system do not allow for a high degree of precision in these definitions, and readers with intimate knowledge of the areas involved will undoubtedly discover anomalies, but the figures do nevertheless convey a good picture of the geographical origins of those attending the meetings.

South-West Area Mission

The South-West Area Mission was held at Ashton Gate football stadium, Bristol. The stylised map shows the approximate limits of each region, and indicates the towns which have been included in each case. It will be noted that the eastern sector of the inner region includes the large town of Bath, whilst the western inner district includes the Welsh hinterland of the Severn Bridge. The outer area includes some other major urban areas, including Gloucester to the north, and Cardiff and Newport to the west. There is also a number of large urban areas immediately beyond the 30 mile radius.

The table indicates that central Bristol produced 13% of the total

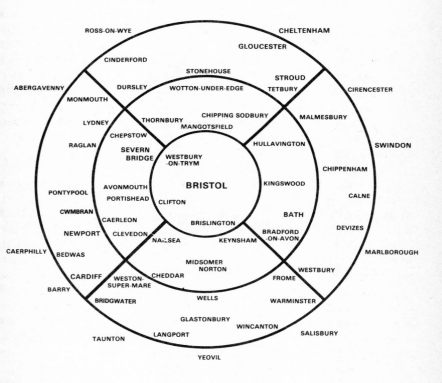

Table 29: Percentage of attendance by direction and distance — Bristol

Percentage of attendance

Central	13%
Inner East	9%
Inner South	9%
Inner West	6%
Inner North	8%
Inner subtotal	32%
Outer East	4%
Outer South	6%
Outer West	5%
Outer North	7%
Outer subtotal	22%
Over 30 miles	33%

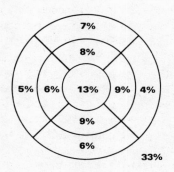

attendance; this is the lowest percentage figure for a central area of any of the six missions. Possible reasons for this are either a lack of support from the inner city area, or alternatively, a proportionately heavier involvement of those outside the immediate urban area than was the case elsewhere. The figures suggest that the latter is much more true at Bristol than was the case anywhere else, and leads to the conclusion that Bristol really was an area rather than a local mission.

One-third of attenders came from the inner area, within 15 miles of the city centre. These were fairly evenly spread between the east, south and northern parts, which include the suburban areas of Kingswood, Keynsham and Mangotsfield respectively, but a smaller number came from the western area around Avonmouth, Portishead, and the Welsh end of the Severn Bridge. The eastern sector is probably the most densely populated, including as it does the substantial city of Bath, and this probably accounts for the higher percentage reported in this district.

Just over one-fifth came from the outer area. Bristol is reasonably well served by motorways in most directions other than to the south east, towards Salisbury and Southampton. The majority of those coming from this distance travelled from the north, which includes Gloucester and Stroud, and from the south which embraces Bridgwater and Weston-super-Mare. The smaller numbers from the outer east region are perhaps a reflection of the rural nature of this area, but the lack of support from the west, which includes the densely populated Cardiff and Newport districts, is rather more surprising.

Of those attending the Bristol missions, 33% came from over 30 miles' distance. This is by far the highest percentage for any of the missions and confirms the view that this particular mission had much more than a purely local character. Bristol's good road links have already been mentioned, and the attendance may also have been boosted by virtue of having been the first of the missions, as well as being the only one within easy reach of the south generally. Large numbers from those towns just beyond the 30 mile limit — places such as Cheltenham, Swindon and Taunton — were perhaps to be expected, and smaller numbers of people also came from Salisbury and Caerphilly. More remarkable, perhaps, is the extent of the attendance from the Exeter area at the furthest reaches of the M5, some 80 miles distance from Bristol, which accounted for around 5% of the total attendance. A much smaller number also

covered a similar distance in travelling from Swansea, while large
numbers were also reported from the Torquay and Plymouth areas
Special recognition must, however, be accorded to the significant
contingent who made the 360-mile round-trip journey from west
Cornwall, particularly Truro and Camborne, and saw many of their
number respond. Groups and individuals also travelled from the
Reading and Bournemouth areas. People were also present from as
far away as Maryport in Cumbria and Canterbury, while a small
number of people made the shorter but much more inconvenient
journey from the Isle of Wight.

North East Area Mission

The North East Area Mission was held at Roker Park, Sunderland
Sunderland forms part of a large conurbation on the north-eastern
coast of England and the stylised map therefore only shows areas to
the north, west and south. The major part of the Tyneside conurba
tion lies to the north of Sunderland, and is included in the inner
north sector; a second large conurbation, in the Cleveland area, lies
some 30 miles to the south, and is included in the outer south sector

As the table shows, 1 in 5 of those attending came from the central
area, which in this case is confined to the city of Sunderland itself
extending to a radius of between 3 and 4 miles from the centre. The
relatively small percentage coming from the central area is perhaps
largely attributable to the limited extent of this area in comparison
with the larger metropolitan areas of Birmingham and Liverpool.

A further 43% came from the inner area, outside Sunderland itself
but within 15 miles of the centre. This fairly high percentage is un
doubtedly due to the proximity of Newcastle upon Tyne, and in fact
20%, or nearly half of these people, came from the northern sector
This means that 1 in 5 of those attending the Sunderland Mission
came from metropolitan Newcastle, and one wonders whether the
organisers might not have expected a higher proportion than this to
have originated from there. The balance of those coming from the
inner area are fairly evenly split between the west, which includes
Chester-le-Street and Washington New Town, and the inner south
including Durham and Peterlee New Town. Both these sectors have
fairly good road links with Sunderland.

Around a quarter of attenders came from between 15 and 30 mile
distance, and two-thirds of these came from the outer south sector

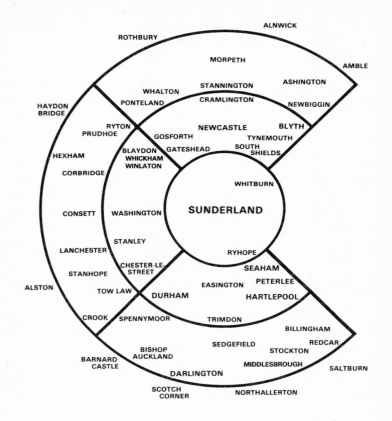

Table 29: *Percentage of attendance by direction and distance — Sunderland*

Percentage of attendance

Central		19%
Inner South	12%	
Inner West	11%	
Inner North	20%	
Inner subtotal		43%
Outer South	18%	
Outer West	5%	
Outer North	4%	
Outer subtotal		27%
Over 30 miles		11%

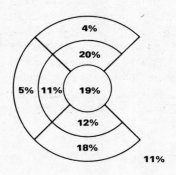

which incorporates the heavily populated Teesside and Darlington areas, and which has good road links with Sunderland. Much smaller numbers came from the outer areas to the west and north of Sunderland, both of which are much more thinly populated, and without such good communications.

Only around one-tenth of those attending the Sunderland mission came from outside the 30-mile radius, representing the smallest proportion of any of the missions. This in part reflects the relative isolation of the north east of the country, cut off as it is by the Yorkshire moors to the south, the Pennines to the west and the Cheviots to the north. Unlike some of the other mission centres, there are few large population centres close to the 30-mile limit, and whilst communications within the north east area are good, there are few good roads leading out of the region.

Of those coming from over 30 miles' distance, the greatest part came from that area of Cleveland which lies just beyond the outer area on the map. Those who did travel from further afield came from York, which has good road links to this area, and also from other parts of Yorkshire such as Beverley and Leeds. A number made the journey from Cumbria, mainly from the area around Carlisle, although there were people there who had made the difficult 100-mile trip from Whitehaven on the Cumbria coast, and a number of other small groups travelled similar distances from Humberside. Individuals were also noted from as far away as Bridgwater in Somerset, and Snodland in Kent.

Sunderland was the nearest that Billy Graham came to Scotland, and it might have been expected that he would draw a noticeable attendance from that part of the country. There were some individuals present from north of the border, including Aberdeen; there was also one from Oban. There was, however, no significant representation at all from Scotland, and although the journey is by no means an easy one, it is perhaps surprising that no-one from Edinburgh appears to have gone forward at the Sunderland Mission.

East Anglia (North) Mission

The East Anglia (North) Area Mission was held at Carrow Road, Norwich. The city of Norwich lies quite near to the eastern coast of England, and the stylised map has therefore required adjustment to

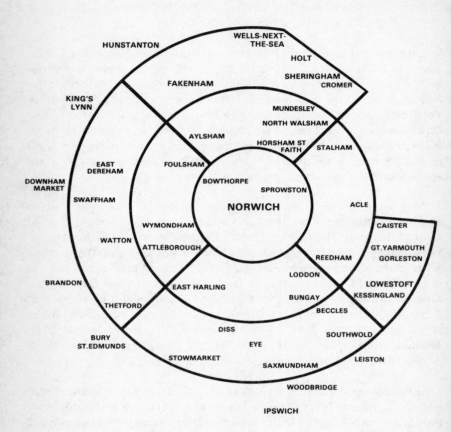

WELLS-NEXT-THE-SEA

HUNSTANTON

HOLT

FAKENHAM

SHERINGHAM
CROMER

KING'S
LYNN

MUNDESLEY

NORTH WALSHAM

AYLSHAM

HORSHAM ST
FAITH

STALHAM

FOULSHAM

EAST
DEREHAM

BOWTHORPE

SPROWSTON

DOWNHAM
MARKET

NORWICH

SWAFFHAM

ACLE

CAISTER

WYMONDHAM

WATTON

ATTLEBOROUGH

GT.YARMOUTH
GORLESTON

REEDHAM

LODDON

LOWESTOFT

BRANDON

EAST HARLING

BUNGAY

KESSINGLAND

THETFORD

BECCLES

DISS

SOUTHWOLD

BURY
ST.EDMUNDS

EYE

STOWMARKET

SAXMUNDHAM

LEISTON

WOODBRIDGE

IPSWICH

Table 31: Percentage of attendance by direction and distance —
Norwich

Percentage of attendance

Central	26%
Inner East	5%
Inner South	9%
Inner West	7%
Inner North	7%
Inner subtotal	28%
Outer East	8%
Outer South	5%
Outer West	6%
Outer North	5%
Outer subtotal	24%
Over 30 miles	22%

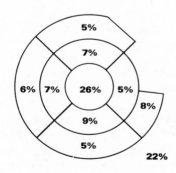

reflect the limited size of the outer areas to the east, in particular, and also to the north. Norwich is itself a smaller town than most of the other mission venues, and forms the focal point of a large rural area with generally low population density. There are no large urban areas within a 30-mile radius of Norwich, and the nearest place of significant size is Ipswich, some 40 miles to the south, where the East Anglia (South) Mission was held later in the year.

The table shows that a quarter of those who attended — about 1 in 4 — came from the city itself, while the remainder were fairly well spread over the immediate surrounding area, the county in general, and even beyond. This Mission's appeal, like that of Bristol, was very much to the area as a whole, although a good response was also evident within the city.

Just over a quarter came from the very rural inner area, which contains no substantial population centres at all. Promoting an event such as Mission England to such a widely dispersed community must have posed some problems to the organisers, but the effort certainly paid off in terms of the attendance from this area. The largest numbers came from the south and north, with smaller groups from the west and the particularly rural east.

A further quarter came from the outer region, of which the largest group came from the outer east sector, which, although small, includes the only towns of any size within the 30-mile limit, namely Great Yarmouth and Lowestoft. Elsewhere, the numbers were fairly evenly spread between the south, west and north.

Just under a quarter of those who attended at Norwich came from over 30 miles away. Although the numbers involved were smaller than at the other missions, the extent of involvement at this distance is surprisingly high considering the relatively poor road system into and within Norfolk. Almost all of those travelling from outside the area came from the Fenlands, and in particular from the areas around King's Lynn, March and Wisbech, although there were other groups from as far as South Lincolnshire. In comparison with other missions, few came from further away, but there were small numbers from Nottingham, and individuals from Blackburn, Newcastle and Newport — no doubt holidaying in the area. The attendance at Norwich was thus very evenly spread across the catchment area with similar proportions from each region.

Midlands Area Mission

The Midlands Area Mission was held at Villa Park, Birmingham. The stylised map shows the densely populated nature of the area immediately surrounding Birmingham, including within the 15-mile radius such substantial population centres as Wolverhampton, Walsall, Dudley, Sutton Coldfield, Coventry and the entire metropolitan area of Birmingham itself. Beyond the 15-mile limit, the area takes on a more rural character, but still includes a number of large towns, particularly in the east, which covers the area of Nuneaton, Rugby and Leamington Spa. It will also be noted that there are a number of large urban areas immediately beyond the 30-mile limit: places such as Derby, Stoke and Leicester.

About a quarter of those attending the Villa Park Mission came from the central district on this map, representing a radius of about 5 miles from the city centre. There was, therefore, a very definite appeal to the city itself as well as to the Midlands area as a whole.

Two of every five attenders came from the inner area; when this is added to the percentage from the centre itself, we note that around two-thirds of the entire attendance at the mission came from within 15 miles of the city centre. Again, two conclusions are possible: either the mission was unable to attract significant numbers from the outer areas, or alternatively it exceeded expectations in terms of its appeal to the metropolis. Given the large numbers which attended the Birmingham meeting, we incline to the latter view; in purely numerical terms the number coming from over 15 miles is comparable to that reported at Bristol.

Although the highest percentage of those travelling from the inner area came from the east, particularly from Coventry, the numbers are fairly evenly spread in all directions, with comparable percentages form the west and south and a slightly smaller proportion from the inner north sector.

Percentages of people travelling from the outer area are correspondingly smaller. Birmingham is well served by motorways, and communication is good in virtually all directions, other than towards Oxford. Again, the highest percentage is recorded for those travelling from the east, which includes Rugby, Nuneaton and Leamington Spa, with the next largest group coming from the outer north sector, around Stafford and Burton upon Trent. The western sector, which has been extended slightly to take in the area of

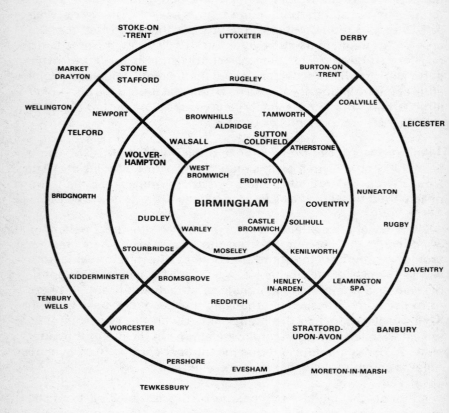

*Table 32: Percentage of attendance by direction and distance —
Birmingham*

Percentage of attendance

Central		26%
Inner East	11%	
Inner South	10%	
Inner West	11%	
Inner North	8%	
Inner subtotal		40%
Outer East	5%	
Outer South	3%	
Outer West	4%	
Outer North	4%	
Outer subtotal		16%
Over 30 miles		18%

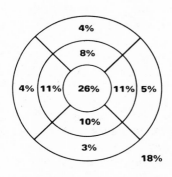

Telford New Town, does not show up particularly well, and one might also perhaps have expected larger numbers from the south where Worcester is within easy motorway reach.

Almost one person in five of those attending the mission travelled more than 30 miles, with most of these coming from Derby, Nottingham and Leicester. Good numbers travelled from Oxfordshire on much slower roads, and there were also groups from areas around the M1, in Northamptonshire, Bedfordshire and Hertfordshire. Four enquirers provided Blackburn postcodes, and individuals were present who gave addresses in Dumfries, Swansea and Southend.

North West Area Mission

The North West Area Mission was held at Anfield stadium, Liverpool. Liverpool is on the west coast of the country, and consequently there is no western sector on the stylised map. The area as a whole is one of dense population, and the map shows a number of large towns within both the 15-mile and 30-mile radius. In the case of Liverpool's outer east region, the boundary has been extended somewhat to take in the whole of the Manchester area, but other parts of Greater Manchester such as Oldham, Stockport and Rochdale have been left outside the 30-mile limit.

It will be noted that almost one-third of the attendance was composed of people living in the densely populated city area of Liverpool itself, which has been taken for this purpose to include the area immediately surrounding the southern end of the Mersey tunnel. This is the highest central area percentage of any of the missions, which is indicative either of the extent to which the mission appealed to the immediate urban area, or alternatively of the failure of the mission to attract people from further afield. The figures suggest in this case that both factors were responsible for the more local character of this mission than, for instance, its Bristol counterpart.

Of those attending, 27% came from within the l5-mile radius. The largest proportion of these came from the area immediately to the north of the city, which includes the suburban areas of Crosby, Kirkby and St Helens along with the holiday resort of Southport and the extensive new town at Skelmersdale. A slightly smaller number came from the area to the south, which comprises the remainder of the Wirral peninsula and the city of Chester, whilst a much smaller percentage came from the inner east region which includes Widnes, Runcorn and the western part of Warrington.

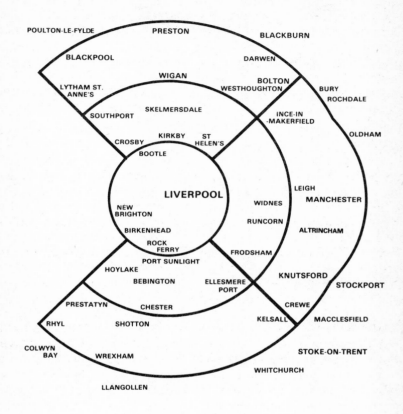

*Table 33: Percentage of attendance by direction and distance —
Liverpool*

Percentage of attendance

Central	30%
Inner East	6%
Inner South	9%
Inner North	12%
Inner subtotal	27%
Outer East	14%
Outer South	3%
Outer North	8%
Outer subtotal	25%
Over 30 miles	18%

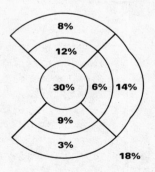

Given the proximity of the heavily populated Manchester area and the quality of road and rail communications between the two major north western cities, we would perhaps expect a fairly high proportion of attenders to come from the outer area. In fact, the Liverpool outer figure of 25% is not particularly high in comparison with those reported from the other missions. Somewhat over half of these did indeed come from the densely populated outer east area, including not only Manchester but also other substantial population centres such as Leigh and Crewe. A good number also came from the outer north, which again incorporates such large urban areas as Blackpool, Preston, Wigan and Bolton. The very small percentage from the outer south is explained by the rural quality of this region, where the largest towns are Wrexham and Rhyl.

The percentage of those who travelled over 30 miles to the Liverpool meetings is 18%. The main sources included the other districts of Greater Manchester — particularly Stockport and Oldham — with significant numbers also travelling from Blackburn and the area around Stoke-on-Trent. Smaller numbers travelled from the Lancaster area, which is linked to Liverpool by motorway, and individuals were recorded from as far away as Aberdeen, Plymouth and Bromley.

East Anglia (South) Area Mission

The East Anglia (South) Area Mission was held at Portman Road, Ipswich. Ipswich is a town of comparable size to Norwich, where the East Anglia (North) Mission was held; it is close to the east coast of the country, and consequently the stylised map shows no outer east sector. The general area to the north, and the inner area as a whole, are predominantly rural in character, but there are some larger urban areas to the south-west, on the approaches to London.

About 1 in 6 of those who went forward at Ipswich were unable to provide satisfactory postcodes, and as with Liverpool, this suggests either a failure on the part of the post office to educate people in this area sufficiently, or a lack of appreciation on the part of counsellors of the importance of this information.

Of those attending the Ipswich mission, 18% came from the central area, which was in this case limited to the city of Ipswich itself. As was the case with the Norwich mission, there was a good spread of attendance across the range of the map and beyond, so again this campaign takes on the character of an area mission. Although the percentage attending from the central area is markedly lower than was the case with the Norwich mission, the number of people originating from the centre is slightly higher for a town of almost identical size.

A quarter of those attending came from the inner area within 15 miles of the city centre. This is a largely rural area, and contains few centres of population. Again, numbers were relatively small, but apparently the mission was effectively publicised in the small and widely dispersed communities around Ipswich. The largest numbers came from the inner south sector, which contains few large settlements, although it does stretch to the borders of Colchester. Numbers from the larger northern sector, and the east which includes the port of Felixstowe, were identical, and there was a smaller percentage from the western sector.

Nearly one-third came from the outer area, these being almost equally divided between the south, which includes the large town of Colchester together with the Essex holiday resorts, and from the west, including Bury St Edmunds, Sudbury and Braintree. Hardly anybody came from the outer north area, which to a large extent overlaps with the outer south sector of the Norwich mission. Generally, those people from this area who attended any mission had already been to the Norwich meetings.

A relatively high percentage, over a quarter, came from beyond 30 miles distance. The largest number of these came from the area of Chelmsford — about 7% of the total attendance — and the majority of the others came from elsewhere in Essex, including a number from Southend-on-Sea. Some people travelled from the Cambridge area, and groups were present from the Air Force Bases at Mildenhall and Lakenheath, where a number of US servicemen are stationed. Ipswich is easily reached from south Essex and Cambridge, and it is not surprising that those who did travel came from this direction. Individuals from further afield gave postcodes indicating residence in Inverness and Carlisle.

One factor which affects only the East Anglia (South) Mission but which may have had a bearing on the distance people travelled is the fact that originally the Mission was scheduled to end on the Friday evening. Consequently, no weekend meetings at all were planned at first, although the Saturday was added later. Those travelling from further afield, therefore, would have had to make

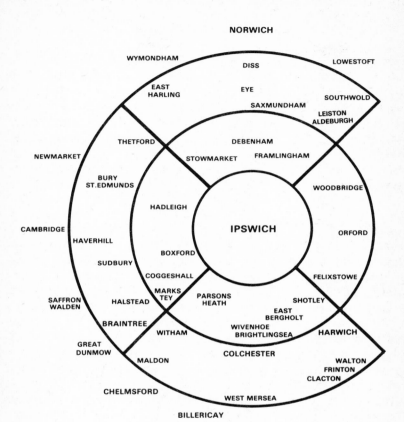

NORWICH

WYMONDHAM

LOWESTOFT

DISS

EAST
HARLING

EYE

SOUTHWOLD

SAXMUNDHAM

LEISTON
ALDEBURGH

THETFORD

DEBENHAM

NEWMARKET

STOWMARKET

FRAMLINGHAM

BURY
ST.EDMUNDS

WOODBRIDGE

HADLEIGH

CAMBRIDGE

IPSWICH

ORFORD

HAVERHILL

BOXFORD

SUDBURY

COGGESHALL

FELIXSTOWE

SAFFRON
WALDEN

MARKS
TEY

PARSONS
HEATH

SHOTLEY

HALSTEAD

EAST
BERGHOLT

BRAINTREE

WIVENHOE
BRIGHTLINGSEA

HARWICH

WITHAM

GREAT
DUNMOW

MALDON

COLCHESTER

WALTON
FRINTON
CLACTON

CHELMSFORD

WEST MERSEA

BILLERICAY

Table 34: Percentage of attendance by direction and distance — Ipswich

Percentage of attendance

Central   18%

Inner East   6%
Inner South   7%
Inner West   5%
Inner North   6%

Inner subtotal   24%

Outer South   15%
Outer West   14%
Outer North   2%

Outer subtotal   31%

Over 30 miles   27%

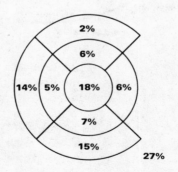

arrangements to attend on weeknights, and this might have discouraged those who had to make long or difficult journeys.

Ipswich is only 80 miles from central London, by far the nearest mission to the capital. It is therefore worth noting that, apart from a few isolated individuals from the outlying north eastern suburbs of London, there was virtually no attendance from the capital. Those who gave London postcodes were in all probability holidaymakers in the Suffolk area. At the time of the Ipswich mission, Mission to London had already finished; nevertheless it appears that by the end of the summer Londoners had had sufficient exposure to the gospel and it is not altogether surprising that they did not go to Ipswich.

Nationwide

It is helpful to compare the distances which people travelled to each of the missions, and the table and diagram below confirm the differing nature of each of the area missions.

In each case, the largest percentage came from within 15 miles' distance of the city centre, but at Bristol and Ipswich the numbers who came from this distance constituted less than half the total attendance. At Bristol in particular, nearly a third of those who attended the mission came from over 30 miles' distance, and of all the missions, Bristol was certainly the one which reached the widest geographical area. Ipswich may also be termed an area mission as nearly 60% of those who attended came from beyond 15 miles' range, with nearly half of these coming from over 30 miles away.

At Norwich, slightly over half the total attendance came from within the 15-mile area, but the percentage of attenders who came from further afield suggests that this mission was also fairly successful in reaching the wider geographical area of Norfolk. The pattern is a little different at Liverpool, although of course the numbers here are in excess of those who attended at Norwich. At Liverpool, a slightly larger percentage came from within the 15-mile area, whilst a smaller proportion came from beyond 30 miles. In the case of Liverpool, however, it should be remembered that the '15 to 30 miles area' has been extended slightly to take in the whole of Manchester, and if we adjust for this, the pattern at this mission is not so dissimilar from that at Norwich.

Table 35: Distances travelled by people attending Mission England

	Within 15 miles	15–30 miles	Over 30 miles	Total
Bristol	45%	22%	33%	100%
Sunderland	62%	27%	11%	100%
Norwich	54%	24%	22%	100%
Birmingham	66%	16%	18%	100%
Liverpool	57%	25%	18%	100%
Ipswich	42%	31%	27%	100%

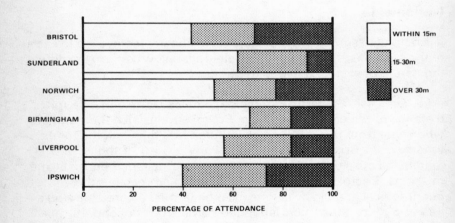

The Birmingham and Sunderland missions are particularly characterised by the very high percentages who came from within the 15-mile area. At Sunderland, 62% of those who attended came from less than 15 miles away, while those travelling from beyond 30 miles form a much smaller percentage than at the other venues. As has already been mentioned, this no doubt reflects the difficulties of communication into the north eastern area of the country. At Birmingham, just about two-thirds of the attenders came from the immediate, urban area, although the percentage of those travelling from over 30 miles' distance is much higher than is the case for Sunderland, and the surprising feature is the small number who travelled from 15 to 30 miles. These last two missions appear to have been much more confined in their impact, although it has to be said that the attendance at Birmingham was much larger, and the percentages for people travelling from further away, whilst relatively small, do nevertheless represent significant numbers of people.

AREAS TOUCHED BY MISSION ENGLAND

As has already been explained, those who came forward at each of the Mission England meetings were asked to supply a postcode, from which we have already suggested the geographical origins of those attending the rallies. The postcode can also be used to demonstrate the extent of response in particular — and quite small — districts of the country, which in turn can provide us with some very important information. Again only the outer elements of the postcode has been used. There are some 2,700 such districts in the country and each outer element thus covers, on average, 8,300 addresses or 90 square kilometres.

In the maps which follow, postcode districts are shaded according to the number of respondents who gave addresses in each. In interpreting these maps, it should be borne in mind that the shading takes no account of the population of a particular postcode district, and care should therefore be taken in comparing the response in one area with that in another, which may have a substantially different population. What can be stated with some confidence is that we would expect to see larger numbers of enquirers from urban postcode areas, and possibly from large rural postcode districts, and that the numbers of respondents would diminish gradually in proportion to the distance from the mission stadium itself. The interest in these maps thus lies in two areas:

Where these expectations are not fulfilled, and where there are exceptions to the pattern that we would expect to see;

Where, irrespective of population density, a large number of people have made a response.

It is important to bear in mind that this type of analysis does not constitute a complete picture. A response of 50 from a small rural community will not necessarily appear on these maps, but in terms of the local population size would represent a revival. It would be impossible to isolate such situations without looking at the more detailed elements of the postcode and thereby breaking the confidence of respondents. The analysis can nevertheless provide some important pointers, and the commentary on each of the maps will endeavour to highlight two features:

> Which areas contain large numbers of people who went forward at Mission England. Particular responsibility rests on the churches and nurture groups in these districts to ensure that the continuing spiritual needs of these people are catered for.

> Which areas within the mission's 'sphere of influence' were left relatively untouched, and consequently constitute a mission field for local churches and evangelists, or indeed future major campaigns.

The question which continues to recur as one examines these maps is this: why should the responsiveness of one postcode district vary so much from others which appear to have similar population size and characteristics? We might rephrase this question by asking why the Holy Spirit touches hearts in one area, and not those in another. It is of course true that 'the wind blows wherever it pleases ... you cannot tell where it comes from or where it is going', but there is also a sense in which the involvement of small Christian groups in prayer, personal witness and transportation arrangements can have a significant influence in preparing the ground for the seed to be sown. There is therefore much to be learned from the maps that follow with details of local church involvement, to determine the relationship that may exist between this and the responsiveness of particular geographical areas.

South West Area Mission

The map for the South West Area Mission contrasts quite dramatically with the other local missions in that the largest numbers of respondents occur not only in the city area itself but also in the surrounding districts. In fact, the highest number of respondents from any postcode district — nearly 600 — occurs in BA2 to the south and south west of Bath. Another significant number from district BA1 gives us a total of precisely 1,000 changed lives in the Bath area alone; given that the average attendance at a church in the area is

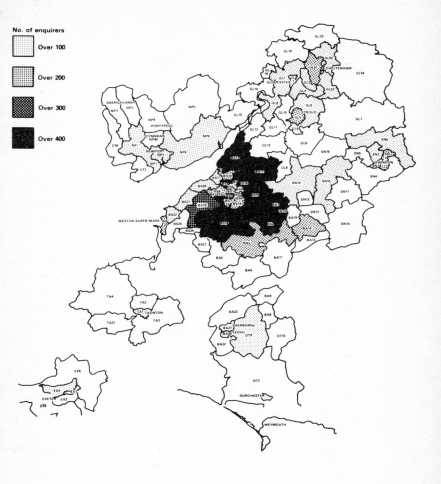

No. of enquirers

□ Over 100

▦ Over 200

▨ Over 300

■ Over 400

101

101, this figure corresponds to almost 10 new churches of average size, and this type of statistic highlights the very dramatic effect of this mission on the Bath area in particular. Another very high number of respondents came from the small but densely populated area of BS16 (Mangotsfield) and 400 or more respondents were also reported in the large rural areas of Avon around Thornbury (BS12), Chipping Sodbury (BS17) and two other areas, which although rural, appear to take in suburbs of the city as well (BS15 and BS18). Another high number of respondents is recorded in BS19 around Nailsea and Yatton. It is thus evident that the response at this mission is by no means confined to a small number of districts; lives have been transformed throughout the inland part of the county of Avon by the message that Billy Graham brought.

Large numbers of respondents are also evident within the city, where they are perhaps more to be expected in view of the population density. The highest numbers came from BS9, with over 500 individuals counselled, and from BS3; only the BS1 and BS2 districts show less than 300 respondents, probably because of the commercial nature of these districts which would mean that fewer people actually live there.

The map also shows that there are some interesting exceptions to the pattern, and to the west of the city the picture is much less dramatic. People from the coastal side of the city did respond, but in much smaller numbers than in the inland districts.

Further afield, some of the major urban areas nearby stand out as one would expect, with large numbers of people in Stroud, Cheltenham, Swindon and Weston-super-Mare. An interesting feature here is that the areas between some of these places and Bristol itself did not show up to any significant extent. In some cases, the difference is marginal — Cirencester (GL7) only just fails to show up on the map, although this is an extremely large district and might be expected to have had a higher number of respondents. Elsewhere, however, the lack of impact is quite remarkable; only 8 respondents gave the postcode GL9 around Badminton, and there were even fewer from GL13 in the vicinity of Sharpness. It is quite remarkable that these areas should have so few respondents when very high numbers of lives were touched in adjacent postcode districts. There is also an evident contrast between the likes of Taunton and Exeter, some considerable distance away, which both show on the map, and Salisbury, where the response was quite limited. District DT9, around Sherborne in Dorset, is an unexpected area which appears to have seen a good response to the gospel.

The effect in Wales is seen to be limited to the Newport and Chepstow areas, and even there is not so great as in the main part of the county of Avon. Perhaps the Welsh felt that a mission specifically directed at England was not intended for them. It is particularly significant that the large and densely populated area of Cardiff was not particularly touched by the mission and does not show up on the map.

North East Area Mission

Attention has been drawn elsewhere to the failure of the Sunderland mission to draw large numbers of people from beyond the immediate area; this map demonstrates that the impact of the mission was limited to a relatively small number of postcode districts in a much more confined area than was the case with the Bristol mission.

The biggest response came from the city of Sunderland itself, where a high response might be expected by virtue of the population density. The area of SR6, which takes in Roker and Whitburn, was particularly affected by the mission, and nearly 700 people from this district alone went forward, the second highest response of any individual postcode district in the entire nation. Two other areas were affected to the extent of over 400 people who went forward — SR4 and SR3 — and only the SR1 area, presumably the commercial centre of Sunderland, has less than 290 respondents. Putting these figures together, we conclude that altogether some 2,200 lives were changed in the Sunderland city area alone, which in terms of the average church size for the area is the equivalent of 14 new churches. It can therefore be claimed with some justification that the town of Sunderland was transformed by the mission, and it is very much to be hoped that the churches in the city can cope with the implications of these numbers.

Given its proximity to Sunderland, and the population density of the area, we would expect a similar, although perhaps slightly smaller, pattern of numbers from the adjacent areas of Newcastle. The map shows that this is not in fact the case, and although a good number of those who went forward came from Newcastle, it is evident that by no means all areas of the city were affected, and indeed only two districts can show more than 200 respondents. One of these is NE34, immediately to the north of Sunderland, and very close to the mission centre itself; in contrast, NE35, 36 and 37, which

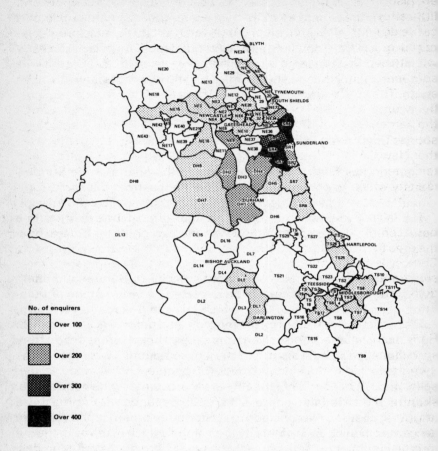

No. of enquirers

Over 100

Over 200

Over 300

Over 400

are also adjacent to Sunderland city, appear to have been relatively little affected by the mission on their doorstep. Other areas of Newcastle do show up on the map, but certainly not to the extent that we might expect given the concentration of population in this area, whilst there is a marked lack of response from NE8 (Gateshead) compared with the adjacent district of NE9 immediately to the south. The area to the north of Newcastle appears to have been relatively untouched, with the exception of Whitley Bay and Earsdon; the same is true of the south west of the city with only a small response from Blaydon, Winlaton, Byker and Ryton. Is it then the case that Newcastle people will not go to Sunderland? The figures certainly tend to support such a view, and it is evident that Newcastle is a city which largely still needs to hear the gospel message.

The lack of response in Newcastle is, to a certain extent, counterbalanced by the large numbers of people touched who came from the area to the west and south-west of Sunderland, particularly from Chester-le-Street and Durham city. A total of 900 people from this small and confined area of the old county of Durham responded during the course of the Sunderland mission.

The pattern in more distant urban areas is mixed. All three Hartlepool postcode districts contain significant numbers of respondents, totalling 440 people, and representing 4 new churches in the town. Slightly further south in Teesside, however, it can be seen that response was patchy — while Thornaby and Stockton show on the map, Middlesbrough and Billingham do not. Further inland, Aycliffe and West Darlington show a level of response which is not matched by the eastern part of Darlington. It is, nevertheless, interesting that the response from these more distant places is of a similar level to that noted in Newcastle, and the effect of the mission on lives in these areas should be a challenge to Newcastle churches, and, indeed, to other relatively untouched areas such as Bishop Auckland, Blyth and Tynemouth.

East Anglia (North) Mission

A smaller number of people went forward at the Norwich mission than at the eight-day missions, and in fact no postcode district contains more than two hundred respondents. Accordingly, the criteria for appearance on the map have been adjusted, and the map shows postcode districts where responses of over 100 and over 50 individuals were reported. It is immediately apparent from the map that

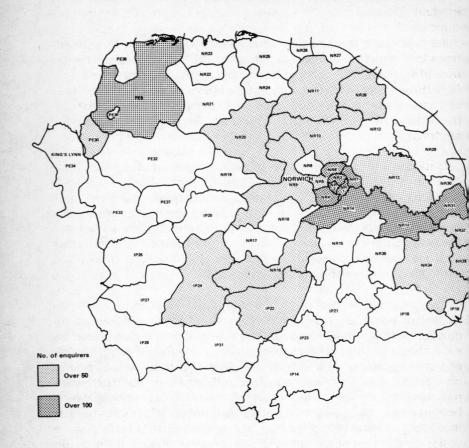

No. of enquirers

Over 50

Over 100

106

only a small number of postcode districts were significantly affected by the Norwich mission, but there are nevertheless some interesting features .

As one would expect, the highest numbers going forward came from the immediate city area, the most affected area being the district of NR3. In suburban areas, a lower response is evident from NR5 (Bowthorpe) than from the other suburbs; an even smaller response is noted for the district of NR8, although it is not clear from the map whether this area includes any significant population centre.

Outside the city of Norwich itself, only three postcode districts can claim more than 100 respondents. Each of these is remarkable. NR14, a large rural area immediately to the south of Norwich, might be expected to contain a large number of respondents, but this does not explain why the adjacent and equally convenient district of NR18 around Wymondham should have been virtually unaffected. There is a similar unexplained contrast between NR14 and the adjacent, although more distant, areas of NR15 and NR35 (Bungay) which failed to show up on the map.

Gorleston-on-Sea (NR31) also shows up as an area significantly touched by the mission. There is a dramatic contrast between this area and NR30 immediately to the north, which includes the large population centre of Great Yarmouth, but which does not show up on the map at all. Those with a more intimate knowledge of the area may care to consider why there should be this dramatic difference between two adjacent towns, and why the number of lives affected in Gorleston was four times the response in Great Yarmouth.

Perhaps most remarkable of all is the rural district of PE71 in northwest Norfolk. To some extent, the number of respondents for this area is explained by its size — it is quite large, although not more so than some other less responsive areas — but it has no population centre of any significance at all. We are unable to determine whether the people affected in this area came from the same community or whether the area as a whole was touched, as this would mean examining the detailed (and thus confidential) elements of the postcode. It is, nevertheless, evident that this area, some considerable distance from Norwich, was dramatically affected by the message Dr Graham brought. The area also stands in contrast to the relatively unaffected districts immediately around it, some closer to Norwich.

The only large population centre in the vicinity of Norwich, with the exception of Great Yarmouth, is Lowestoft, and a number of people from this town were touched, although it has to be said that the response is not particularly high in terms of the size of population in the area. The same is true of the much more distant town of Kings Lynn. Norwich is surrounded by a number of small towns, and many of these appear to have been left virtually unaffected by the mission. The areas around Thetford, Diss and East Harling are highlighted on the map, but relatively few respondents came from Wymondham, Bungay, East Dereham, Sheringham or Cromer. There certainly would appear to remain a wide field for mission in the smaller towns of Norfolk.

Midlands Area Mission

As is the case with most of the other missions, the districts with the highest numbers of respondents are those densely populated urban districts close to the mission venue. The map confirms that the response was generally good throughout the West Midlands area, but there are nevertheless some interesting contrasts between districts.

The highest individual response came from those living in postcode district B6, in the very centre of Birmingham, where 440 of those who went forward have their homes. The adjacent areas of B20 and B23 can also claim high numbers of respondents, and between them these three areas contain almost 1,200 people who went forward at the mission. If none of these was already church attenders, this figure represents the equivalent of 10 new churches of average size in this very small area of the city. Many other postcode districts of the city have over 200 people who went forward, and most parts of the urban area were touched to some extent, but there are nevertheless some places where the numbers are too low to show up on the map. The small number of respondents from B1–5 can probably be explained by the preponderance of commercial property in this area, but the lack of significant numbers of respondents from B9, B10, B25, B34, B35 and B72 form a ring which stands in marked contrast to the areas which they encircle, each of which has a high number of respondents. What characteristics of these postcode districts would explain the lack of response to the gospel in these areas?

Other interesting patterns can be seen further out in the suburbs and other large urban areas close to Birmingham. Large numbers of

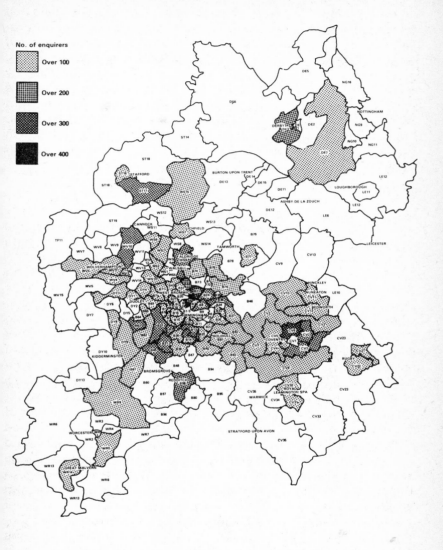

No. of enquirers

Over 100
Over 200
Over 300
Over 400

people in the southern suburbs responded, but the response to the north and west of the city, in Dudley, Wolverhampton and Walsall was much more mixed. In each of these towns, some areas appear to have been effectively reached, whilst others are relatively untouched. West of Birmingham, for example, a good number of people from Halesowen were counselled, but relatively few from Brierley Hill. The same is true in Wolverhampton, where WV10 had a large number of people counselled, but adjacent districts show no significant level of response at all, while to the north the high number of respondents in Aldridge (WS9) contrasts sharply with the lack of response from people living in central Walsall. Again, it is intriguing to find this type of pattern; it would be extremely interesting to explore the background to the differing impact of the gospel on different parts of the area.

East of Birmingham, the large urban area of Coventry shows the expected high level of response, though it is worth noting that the area CV6 to the north of the city centre contains more respondents than most postcode districts in Birmingham itself, and that high numbers are also noted in CV2 and CV3 to the east and south of the city centre. Altogether, over 1,300 people from Coventry and its immediate suburbs went forward at the mission, and these would constitute another 11 new churches in the city. The mission also appears to have had a significant effect in the region around Coventry and other urban areas like Rugby and Leamington Spa also show up on the map. Contrasts are again self-evident; while Leamington Spa shows perhaps the expected pattern of response, the adjacent town of Warwick fails to do so, and while Nuneaton is highlighted, the adjacent town of Hinckley is not.

South of the city, it is interesting to compare the high number of respondents from B98 (the new town of Redditch) with the lack of a sizable response from residents of Bromsgrove (B60) or indeed anywhere else in that general area. South-east Worcester and Great Malvern are also areas which have been affected by the mission, but a number of nearer towns, some of which form part of large postcode areas, fail to appear as prominently as might be expected. The lack of impact of the mission is particularly noticeable in places such as Kidderminster, Stourport and Stratford-upon-Avon. A similar situation is evident to the north of Birmingham, where two areas appear to have been particularly touched: DE3 to the west of Derby and ST17 to the south and south-west of Stafford, with response noted also in Stafford itself, Rugeley, and the large rural postcode district of DE7 in south Derbyshire. It is curious, therefore, that closer population centres such as Lichfield, Tamworth and Burton-upon-Trent have not been particularly touched by the mission, and one might also have expected a much higher response from the area of Telford New Town in the area to the north-west of Birmingham. It is also noted that no postcode district in Leicestershire is highlighted on the map at all, although in fairness it should be mentioned that LE8 (to the south of Leicester itself) has 99 people who went forward in the course of the Birmingham mission.

North West Area Mission

Attention has already been drawn elsewhere to the large percentage of those attending the Liverpool mission who came from the city of Liverpool itself. The map shows that many districts of the city have large numbers of residents who responded at the mission, and again this conforms to the expected pattern of high numbers of respondents in densely populated areas. What is not satisfactorily explained is the exceptionally high number of respondents (837) from the L4 postcode district of Anfield, the highest number of respondents from any individual postcode area in the entire country. If none of these poeple were already church attenders, then an additional four churches of average size would be required within an area of only a few square miles, which now also contains 465 new Christians as a result of Mission England. The character of the area can only have been transformed by what has taken place in the lives of its residents.

Although the response in L4 was twice as high as that of the residents of any other postcode area, numbers of over 400 were also reported in L25, (Walton), and in the suburban area of L63 (Bebington, in the Wirral). Other areas with high numbers of respondents included L5 and L6 in the city of Liverpool itself, L23 (Crosby), L43 (part of Birkenhead) and L20 (Bootle). Most areas of the city itself were touched to some extent, with the exception of L1–3 which are almost certainly dominated by commercial property; other postcode districts in the city area itself which do not appear to have been significantly affected were L10, the small area of L28, and L26 and L24 to the south east of the city.

In the suburban areas around Liverpool, the area to the north and east of the city shows a pattern of consistently high response, stretching in a band from Southport through Formby, Ormskirk, Skelmersdale, Rainford, Warrington, and Widnes to Runcorn. All

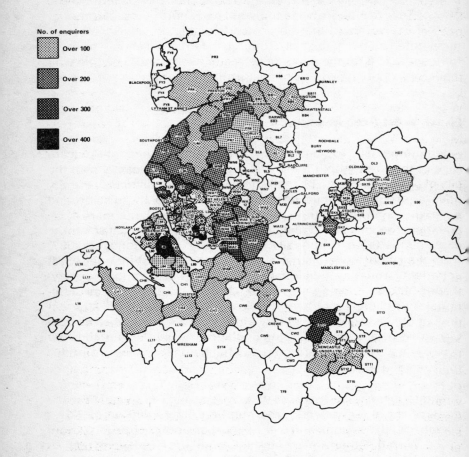

No. of enquirers

Over 100

Over 200

Over 300

Over 400

these districts show significant numbers of people who went forward, as do the areas around Preston and Blackburn further north. There is a contrast between these districts and those around Wigan, Leigh and south and east Bolton, where no significant number of people was reached.

In the Wirral, the response in Birkenhead was generally good, and the numbers of people touched in the Bebington area have already been mentioned. These areas contrast sharply with Hoylake and West Kirkby, and also Ellesmere Port, which were relatively unaffected. In North Wales, more people from the rural area around Mold and Buckley responded than their counterparts from the more populous coastal area, or from Wrexham. Those parts of Cheshire closest to Liverpool saw some response, but the mission had relatively little impact around Crewe or Macclesfield; on the other hand, unexpectedly large numbers of people from the Alsager/Kidsgrove area went forward, and the response from the Five Towns area was generally good.

Most noticeable of all, however, is the almost total lack of impact of the mission on any postcode district in Manchester. Only one district can claim more than 100 respondents, this being the area of Denton (M34). The counsellor forms tell us that a number of Manchester people attended the rallies, and went forward, but the map certainly indicates that the numbers who did so were not of the order that might have been expected given the population density of this area. It is therefore important to bear in mind for future campaigns of this type that Manchester has been left relatively untouched by what has taken place in 1984. There are, of course, exceptions, and Cheadle (SK8) stands out particularly; why should more than 200 residents of this area have gone forward, when fewer than 100 from anywhere in Manchester did so? The Hyde and Romiley districts of Stockport — whose inhabitants had to travel through Manchester to reach Liverpool — also show up on the map, but other areas of Greater Manchester such as Oldham, Rochdale, and Bury were relatively unaffected.

East Anglia (South) Mission

As with the Norwich mission, the map has been adjusted to show those postcode districts where more than 50 residents responded to the gospel message.

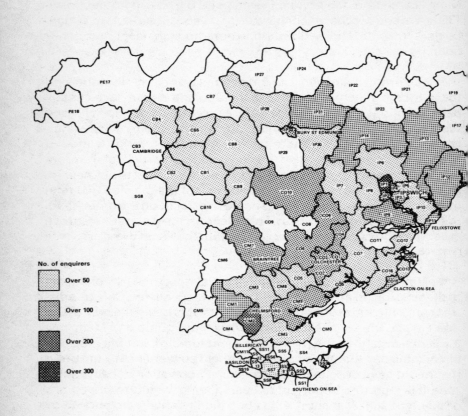

No. of enquirers

Over 50

Over 100

Over 200

Over 300

As might have been expected, the highest numbers of respondents came from the city of Ipswich itself, particularly IP1 with over 350 residents who went forward. High numbers of respondents are also evident from IP2 and IP4, while the IP3 district is only just below 200. On the other hand, IP5 to the east of Ipswich barely shows at all on the map. Altogether, around 1,100 people from Ipswich went forward at the rally, almost 1% of the population of the city, and it is evident that the city of Ipswich was greatly affected by the message that was preached there. The average attendance at a Suffolk church is 77 people, and in those terms the response in Ipswich is the equivalent of 14 new churches.

Elsewhere, the concentration of numbers is evident around the urban area of Colchester, with the exception of the small CO1 postcode district which is probably a commercial area with few residents. The response rate from the Colchester area does however appear to be much lower than in Ipswich. The surprising feature of the map is possibly the level of response from Chelmsford, where the CM2 postcode district shows the fourth highest response of all in this area. Chelmsford is a smaller town than Colchester, and being further away might have been expected to show a lower number of respondents, so it is interesting that residents of this town should have responded in such large numbers.

Most other towns in the area show up on the map to a greater or lesser extent. Clacton, Maldon, Braintree, Sudbury and Bury St Edmunds all have more than 100 residents who went forward, as does the port of Felixstowe to the south east of Ipswich. Across the Stour estuary at Harwich, a town of similar size, the response was markedly smaller, and the number of residents of this area who went forward was in fact less than half the number of Felixstowe residents who did so. This may simply reflect the fact that the number of people from Harwich who actually attended was smaller due to the lack of good communications and the more difficult journey involved.

In the rural areas, it is interesting that the districts immediately around Ipswich have a lower response than their more distant counterparts. The notable exception is the rural district of IP9 to the south of the city, with no population centre of any size, where more than 100 people went forward. It is difficult to comment meaningfully on the contrast between the areas immediately around Ipswich and those further away without knowledge of the population involved; the more distant districts seem on the whole to be larger in area.

Significant numbers of respondents can be noted at a considerable distance from the mission centre itself. Southend, Newmarket and Cambridge all have over 50 residents who went forward, and so does the postcode district of IP28 centred on the Air Force base at Mildenhall. Lakenheath, on the other hand, shows a much lower number of respondents, although the figures suggest that those who did attend Mission England from this area went to Ipswich rather than Norwich.

Given the level of response from quite distant areas, it is perhaps surprising that closer rural areas, and in particular CO9 around Halstead, should not show up on the map as having been affected by the mission. The apparent lack of response in the northern part of the county, however, is explained by its proximity to Norwich, and the fact that those who went to Mission England from these areas tended to gravitate towards the north rather than the south. The only area of any overlap is IP21, a rural area east of Diss, which does not show up on either map but where the combined response at Norwich and Ipswich exceeded 50 residents.

CONCLUSION

We may summarise the main findings of the research as follows:

— Over a million people attended Mission England meetings, representing one in fifty of the population of England and Wales. On average, over 25,000 attended each meeting.

— One in eleven of those who attended went forward for further counselling. On average over 2,300 responded at each meeting.

— The best attended meetings were those held on Fridays and Wednesdays.

— Sunday was the least well attended day, and also saw the lowest level of response — perhaps because more Christians were present.

— Youth emphasis nights achieved above-average attendance and response levels, particularly from young people. This was particularly true for youth emphasis nights on Fridays.

— Weather may have affected attendance to a limited extent, particularly at Sunderland.

— The message theme which drew the best response overall was 'The value of a soul' (Mark 8:31–38).

— Well over half of those who went forward wished to accept Jesus Christ as Saviour. One in six sought to renew a prior commitment to Christ.

— If we assume that none of those who accepted Christ already attended church, this is the equivalent of 400 new churches of average size in England, or 10 new churches for each Mission England meeting.

— People from all age-groups, all occupational and denominational backgrounds responded. Age was the most important factor in determining response: two-thirds of the under-18s who responded accepted Christ, but less than half the adults did so. Sex, occupation and denominational background also had bearings on the types of response made.

— Over half the enquirers were aged 18 and under, as against only one in five of the general population.

— Half of those accepting Christ were aged between 11 and 18, while less than one-third of those rededicating themselves came from this age-group.

— Three women responded for every two men, on average, but the proportions were five to four among children and three to one among old age pensioners. There was a significant fall in response among men over the age of 25.

— Students were by far the largest occupational group, followed by homemakers, and then the unemployed and industrial workers.

— Almost half of the enquirers claimed association with the Church of England. The other denominations best represented were Methodists and Baptists.

— At the local missions:

> Birmingham, Liverpool and Bristol were best attended. Liverpool, Birmingham and Sunderland saw the greatest response.

> Birmingham, Liverpool and Sunderland experienced the largest percentage of enquirers accepting Christ; the largest proportions rededicating themselves were seen at Norwich and Bristol.

> The denominational background of enquirers varied by location, but other characteristics varied much less.

> One in three of those attending at Bristol travelled over 30 miles; only one in ten at Sunderland came that far. Two-thirds of those attending at Birmingham came from within 15 miles of the city centre.

The response from particular postcode districts varied dramatically. Most significantly, Manchester and (to a lesser extent) Newcastle were not reached to the degree that might have been expected. Other areas saw an unexpectedly large response in comparison with similar nearby districts.

There are, then, nearly a hundred thousand people in England and Wales today who responded to the challenge posed at Mission England meetings. This statistic testifies to a God who answers prayer — the prayers of the organisers, of course, for the event as a whole, but also the prayers of individual Christians across the country for unsaved and backslidden friends. It also testifies to a God who can do 'immeasurably more than all we ask or imagine' (Eph 3:20). And yet it cannot be left there. These hundred thousand need the love, fellowship and nurture of English Christians and churches if they are to grow in their new faith; and there are still millions of others as yet unreached, needing to hear the gospel message.

Mission England meetings have shown that, even in today's Britain, the gospel is still the power of God for salvation; it has also shown the dimension of the harvest still waiting to be reaped.

UK Christian Handbook
1985/86 Edition

'I have been surprised and delighted, in leafing through the *UK Christian Handbook*, to see the wealth of information which it contains.' LORD DONALD COGGAN

The *UK Christian Handbook* is the only volume listing virtually all Christian organisations in the United Kingdom. For this edition every single entry has been updated, and hundreds added. For ease of reference it has been carefully and thoroughly reorganised after a wide survey of customers' needs.

Do you want a phone number? An address? The name of a chief executive? Turnover? The aims, publications or staff of a given group? Look it up in the *UK Christian Handbook*. It includes bookshops, missionary societies, youth organisations, denominational headquarters, children's homes, retreat and conference centres, relief agencies, adoption agencies, theological colleges, publishers, art and layout services, video producers, tour operators and many more. User aids include a variety of maps and contents indexed by person, location and organisation.

'You can survive in Christian work without the *UK Christian Handbook*—but you'll always be borrowing somebody else's.' GILBERT W. KIRBY

Published jointly with the Evangelical Alliance and Bible Society.

Priced at £10.95

Mission to London Phase 2— Who Went Forward?

During six weeks in the summer of 1984 a quarter of a million people — 1 in 25 of the population of inner London — came to hear Luis Palau present the Christian Gospel at the Queen's Park Rangers Stadium. How did they react? What affected their response? How old were they? Did more women than men respond? Where did the vast crowds come from?

Peter Brierley's carefully researched report provides detailed insights. Supporting his findings with statistics and clearly presented diagrams, he explores the essential characteristics of the 16,000 people who publicly went forward at the meetings.

Peter Brierley has edited many other reference books including the *UK Christian Handbook* and *Prospects for Scotland*. He worked previously for the Bible Society and now serves as European Director of MARC Europe.

Priced at £2.25

Prospects for Scotland

A unique study of church life in Scotland in the 1980s.

This comprehensive survey of church attendance in Scotland was undertaken in March 1984 by The National Bible Society of Scotland and MARC Europe. There was very wide support, and the high response rate — 75% overall — shows that the churches recognised the importance of this census. Without firm facts we have no objective basis for action or policy.

Prospects for Scotland gives us the most accurate picture yet of church attendance patterns in Scotland at a given time. It highlights trends, and shows regional church attendance by sex, age and denomination.

What are some basic lessons?
   * 17% of the adult population of Scotland attend church every week. This is considerably higher than England (9%) or Wales (13%).
   * More churches are growing than declining.
   * Overall attendance declined by 3% between 1980 and 1984, but this is slower than the decline in membership (5%), suggesting that those who do attend are becoming more committed.
   * There were more children in church in 1984 than there were in 1980 in relation to the proportion of children in the civil population.

This study is for all who care about the future of the church in Scotland. If you are a minister, a youth leader, an administrator or have any responsibility for planning, then you will need the information presented here.

Published jointly with The National Bible Society of Scotland.

Priced at £5.95